LILY BALDWIN

The Renegade, Rebel Hearts Series,
Book One

D1707487

# Contents

# Chapter One

Rife with danger and wicked salaciousness, Lady Elora Brodie had never walked the narrow roads and alleyways of Edinburgh's shipyards, nor had she ever imagined she would, especially after nightfall.

"My lady, forgive me but I fear for yer safety," the head of her guard said in a low voice at her side. "Do not think yer title will save ye here."

"Declan, no one knows who I am, nor will they, allowing ye stop calling me my lady," she hissed in reply.

"'Tis not too late to turn back."

She stopped in her tracks and looked her loyal warrior straight on. The silver at his temples shone in the lantern light as did the worry in his gaze. "My mind is made up. I will not be persuaded from my chosen course."

Declan's gaze scanned the Heavens. "There's no moon nor any stars to be seen. 'Tis a bad omen."

She cocked a brow at him. "'Tis dry at least, which I believe is a good omen, considering that it has done naught but rain these last two days."

"Or...mayhap 'tis only the calm before the storm."

She took a deep breath to quiet her frustration. "Declan, ye've been more of a da to me than my father ever was in life. I love ye, and I love how much ye care. But I will command ye back to the livery if ye cannot accept why I've come here."

His eyes flashed wide. "Ye wouldn't wander these streets alone, surrounded as we are by thieves and beggars and whores?" His voice had risen to mirror his concern.

"Wheest," she hissed. "Remember, we do not wish to draw attention our way."

She pressed her lavender-scented handkerchief to her nose, trying, with no avail, to mask the pungent scent of low-tide, dead fish, and other odors she dared not consider long enough to identify. Lantern and torch fire illuminated the motley assortment of people milling about near the docks in varying stages of intoxication. Her surroundings were unnerving, to say the least, but her humble clothing bolstered her confidence. She wore an unadorned dark-green tunic and a simple black cloak, both of which she had borrowed from her maid, Mary. Even Elora's waist-length golden curls had been coaxed into two thick plaits down her back rather than the intricate style and veils that she typically wore. More than that, riding for two days in the rain had left her garments splattered with mud, allowing her to hope that she truly did appear as common as any of the women passing by.

"Ye're a handsome one, aren't ye?"

Elora turned to see who spoke. Her eyes widened when she saw a woman with unbound black hair that fell in ragged waves to her waist pursing her brightly painted lips at Declan. "I'll treat ye right," she crooned, fluttering her lashes.

Elora cringed inwardly as she looked at the woman whose bosom was barely covered by the deep cut of her tunic, over which her tattered surcote was cinched tight to accentuate her ample curves.

Well, mayhap, Elora hoped, she didn't look *that* common.

Declan cleared his throat. "Move along," he replied firmly.

With a shrug, the woman sauntered away, continuing her search for a man to fill her bed and subsequently her purse. Despite her easy laughter, Elora could sense the woman's desperation. In fact, everywhere she turned, she glimpsed regret and grief sadly pushing through smiles meant to hide the pain of the downtrodden and broken-hearted.

Pulling her cloak tighter about her shoulders, Elora forced her gaze back to the roadside where she scanned the businesses lining the narrow, muddy streets. There was a sailmaker and a smithy, both boarded up for the night. Farther down, she spied an apothecary, which was also closed, but in front of the locked entry stood a boy with no more than ten and two years. He had tangled dark hair, a dirty face, and was selling hot pig's feet.

"My—," Declan began but corrected himself by calling her by her given name. "Elora, now that ye've seen this place, surely ye wish to leave and find a comfortable inn. On the morrow, we can seek out the guilds and find a merchant or another tradesman."

Squaring her shoulders, she shook her head firmly in reply. She was very aware of the fact that she did not have the captain's approval, only his protection. Her steward also did not support her decision, but it mattered naught. After all, she was lady of Castle Bròn. She made her own choices, which was exactly the intended goal of her current mission—to maintain control of her own life.

Picking her way carefully down the muddy roads, she forced her attention away from the respectable businesses to the taverns and brothels, all of which looked the same to her...

raucous dens where only the basest of pleasures could find satisfaction.

"Choose one," she muttered to herself, but she knew why she delayed in making her choice.

She was afraid.

Steeling her shoulders, she tilted her chin. This was not her first taste of fear nor would it be her last. Seizing her courage, she took another deep breath and picked a tavern at random.

"The Ship," she declared, looking pointedly at the drinking house across the way where a wooden sign carved with a square-masted cog hung.

Declan opened his mouth as if to try to persuade her once more from her current course, but then he sighed and shook his head. At length, he said, "As ye wish, my lady."

Forcing one foot in front of the other, she approached the slatted door. Just as she reached for the handle, it flung wide. Stepping back quickly, she barely missed being struck in the face by the wood. Raucous laughter and music filtered out on the heels of an old man with wizened cheeks. He stumbled drunkenly into the night. Teetering to the left, he collided into Elora. She gasped, feeling her feet slide out from under her in the slick mud, but Declan seized her arm to keep her upright.

"Where's my ship?" the man slurred, meeting Elora's gaze. Then a slow smile spread across his face, revealing the few remaining teeth he still possessed. "Ye're a pretty bit of skirt."

"Move along," Declan snapped at the old sailor.

Eyes wide, the old man looked up at Declan and nodded, then stumbled backward. When he had crossed the road, Declan whirled to face her, his face etched with concern. "I beg ye to reconsider yer plan. 'Tis too dangerous!"

"The risk is necessary," she shot back. Then she smoothed

her hands down her simple tunic and adjusted her cloak about her shoulders. Certainly, she acknowledged the risks she took. Still, whatever ill she faced in that moment or the days to follow could never compare to the lifetime of unhappiness she was fighting like hell to overcome.

Her plan, although perilous, was simple enough. She needed to hire a man—but not just any man. She had a list of criteria, all of which had to be met.

She needed a man who could be bought, who was not overly concerned with his mortal soul, and who was not without connections. He needn't be a laird or a laird's son, but mayhap a laird's nephew or even an ill-favored cousin. Certainly, such a man may prove difficult to find, but she did not doubt that with persistence and courage, she would complete her mission.

"Trust me, Declan. I know what I'm doing."

She scanned the road ahead and set her gaze on a tavern called, The Devil's Bridge.

Once again, she drew a deep breath, then marched across the road, determined to enter the bawdy establishment regardless of what obstacles she met along the way.

Declan reached the door first. "Please, my lady. Allow me to at least make a quick scan of the room."

Singing, raucous laughter, and raised voices carried outside. She raised her brow at him. "Listen to the din. Ye know very well what it will be like behind that door, and no amount of inspection is going to make ye feel better about me going inside or my purpose for doing so."

Declan's lips pressed together in a grim line. She could almost feel the rebuttals reverberating on the tip of his tongue, but he swallowed his refusals, and instead dipped his head, acknowledging her authority. "Aye, my lady."

Opening the door, he began to step out of the way, but then he stopped and turned on her. His wide shoulders filled the doorway, blocking her entry. Uncharacteristically, he seized her by the arms. "Ye needn't fear Laird Mackintosh's coming. Yer warriors would consider it an honor to die in battle for ye if need be."

She shook her head. "No one is going to die. Now, step aside."

His nostrils flared. She knew it pained Declan, but he did as she bade.

Men crowded around tables, calling out to each other over games of dice. Victors raised their tankards high, sloshing ale on the floor and tabletops while losers cursed and guzzled their cups to soothe the sting of an ill-fated roll. Everywhere, women moved among the tables, serving ale and bowls of pottage, or they perched on men's laps, locked in passionate embraces. Breasts were fondled. Skirts pushed past their knees. Elora gulped. Took another deep breath and squared her shoulders.

It was now or never...

"For the last time, Elora," Declan pleaded in a hushed voice. "A place like this will be crawling with the most disreputable men."

"Good," she said with false confidence as she stepped inside. "Because I am not looking for a reputable man."

# Chapter Two

Nathan Campbell scanned the crowded tavern from where he sat at a corner table. The room stretched out in front of him. The bar was just to his left, and beyond that he could see the stairs leading to the upper level. Across the room to the right, he had a clear view of the doorway; that is, until a comely pair of nearly bare breasts appeared in front of him. Shifting his gaze higher, he locked eyes with a serving wench. She licked her lips suggestively before setting a tankard of ale in front of him.

"Here ye are, lover," she crooned in a husky voice full of longing.

Slowly, seductively, she slid onto the bench beside him. Her full lips pressed against his neck. Then she nibbled her way teasingly to his ear while her hand moved slowly up his bare thigh under the folds of his plaid. His body responded to her touch, lengthening, hardening. With her other hand, she cupped his cheek and boldly kissed him. Tasting sweetness on her tongue, he deepened their kiss, pulling her onto his lap, but he kept his gaze trained on the door. Her breaths quickened. She twisted the fabric of his tunic in her fists as she moaned and squirmed. Skillfully, he stroked her breasts, rubbing her nipples through her threadbare tunic, which grew taut beneath his touch. Arching her back, she pressed her bountiful curves against him.

"Take me upstairs," she begged softly in his ear. "Please, Nathan."

With a simple shake of his head, he seized her lips again, kissing her to silence her pleas. He did not intend to leave the room; at least, not until his business was complete. Ever vigilant, he continued to watch the door for his newest prize, despite the pleasing wench doing everything within her power to distract him.

He stiffened when the door swung wide. Anticipating the arrival of a so-called giant named Bowie—with massive shoulders, shorn blond curls and a jagged scar running from his right eye to his hard, square jaw—Nathan pulled his lips free and angled his head so that he gazed sidelong at the door. But a man of reasonable height and dark hair filled the entryway, oddly with his back to the room. He appeared to be conversing with someone still outside.

Tensing, Nathan shifted the barmaid off his lap.

She pouted in protest. "There isn't a woman in this room who will take care of ye like I will."

"I'm not waiting for a woman," he replied absently, keeping his gaze trained on the door.

"Good," she crooned. He could hear the smile in her voice before she nuzzled her face into his neck and stroked her hand slowly, possessively down his hard length.

Despite her tender administrations, he straightened in his seat when the man stepped aside, and a stunning woman walked into The Devil's Bridge. Her golden hair shimmered in the glow of candlelight. Her features were delicate, her neck long and slender, but it was her bearing that captured his interest. She stood tall, her back poker straight while she scanned the room, her expression impassive. The authority in her stance and the attentiveness of her guard belied her simple garb. Her emotionless gaze passed his corner of the room and they locked eyes. She held his gaze for a stony moment, then turned away and continued her perusal of the busy tavern.

Intrigued, Nathan continued to watch her, and he wasn't alone. Several of the men in the room were neglecting their tankards and the warm, willing women in their arms to marvel at the newcomer's beauty. But despite her apparent charms, no one approached her. Certainly, the seasoned warrior at her side was, in part, to blame, but Nathan believed her stern bearing was the true reason. She was aloof and completely unreadable—at least, at first glance. What no one else might have noticed was her fisted hands. Her white knuckles revealed either the anger or trepidation she so skillfully masked behind her cool façade.

After several moments, her guard leaned close and said something for her ears alone. She gave the slightest nod of her head in acknowledgement. Then she lifted the hem of her mud-splattered tunic and glided across the room to an open table in the corner opposite his own.

He couldn't help but smile when, for the first time since entering the drinking house, her face clearly revealed her thoughts. Like any arrogant and haughty lady might do, she wrinkled her nose at the overturned tankard on the table in disgust. In a flash, her guard snatched up the remains of the table's former occupants and hastened the empty vessels to the bar. Meanwhile, the woman, who he had no doubt was of noble birth, removed a handkerchief from her sleeve and used it to wipe the bench before she sat down, causing Nathan's smile to widen.

As if sensing his amusement, she turned and, once more, met his gaze. With her flaxen hair and flawless white skin, she was as beautiful as freshly fallen snow on the moors and equally as cold. Her eyes showed no warmth. Her movements were controlled and stiff. She was more a finely made statue than a flesh and blood woman in Nathan's eyes.

A gust of wind blew through the tavern as the door once more swung wide, drawing his gaze. In walked a massive man whose hair, size, and scar puckering the skin on his cheek fit the description of the thieving murderer Nathan and his men had been hired to capture.

"'Tis about time," Nathan said before downing the rest of his ale. Then he kissed the warm, red-blooded wench at his side. Sliding out from behind the table, he cracked his knuckles.

"Bowie Mackenzie," he called, thundering across the room to confront the much larger man.

Silence fell over the tavern.

"Who wants to know?" Bowie replied, crossing his thick arms over his muscular chest.

Nathan took a piece of parchment from his sporran. "Laird Cumming wants a word with ye, and he's paid me a small fortune to make certain he has his chance." Nathan held the paper up showing Bowie the Cumming's seal.

A slow smile stretched across Bowie's face, still handsome, despite the thick red line marring one side. "Think ye that I will just surrender and let ye take me?"

Nathan smiled. "A man can hope."

The smile vanished from Bowie's face. "Ye'd best start praying instead."

The giant withdrew the sword strapped to his back. An instant later, the tavern's revelers scurried back, knocking over chairs and tables in their haste to escape the sudden fray.

"Amen," Nathan replied, his voice deadly soft.

With a growl, Bowie attacked. Nathan ducked beneath the might of the giant's first swing, then charged forward, keeping low, and drove his shoulder into Bowie who stumbled back but kept his footing. Again, Bowie thrust his sword at Nathan who sidestepped, avoiding the assault before striking out with his fist and catching Bowie in the nose. A satisfying snap rent the air. Bowie growled as blood gushed from his nostrils. He charged at Nathan, swinging his blade. Nathan ducked and caught Bowie in the jaw with a left hook, followed by a swift punch to the gut. Then he barreled into the larger man, knocking him to the ground. Sprawled on top of the accused criminal, no sooner did Nathan ready his fist to strike Bowie again, than the tips of three swords appeared, all poised a breath away from Bowie's throat.

"Ye weren't supposed to attack until we returned," Caleb, Nathan's partner, snapped.

Nathan shrugged up at his scowling friend. "Ye were late."

Caleb's dark brow furrowed over his clear blue eyes. "We brought our horses to the livery. Ye knew we would not be long."

Nathan lifted his shoulders. "Aye, but he arrived, which means ye were late." Nathan climbed to his feet and looked down at the man whose bloodied face was twisted in rage.

"Laird Cumming is a liar. I stole nothing and killed no one," Bowie snarled, lifting his head and shoulders as if to rise.

"Don't move or I'll slit yer throat," Caleb said, pressing his blade harder against the wanted-man's throat.

Nathan grabbed two coils of rope from Caleb's satchel and tied Bowie's hands together and then his feet. He stared down at the giant whose handsome features had suddenly softened, and for a moment, Nathan saw what lived inside Bowie—fear and hope.

His gaze sought Nathan's. "I'm innocent," he said in a low voice.

Every wanted-man who Nathan had tracked down all made the same claim. "That is for ye and Laird Cumming to work out. My part in this is done." Nathan turned to the other two members of his band of thief-takers. "Bring him to the sheriff and give him this," he said, handing over the sealed orders to William, an older man of few words with a long gray beard and only one eye.

After William tucked the square of parchment into his sporran, Nathan shifted his gaze to Thomas, who, at just ten and six, was the newest and youngest member of their gang. "After he is secured, then ride north to Cumming territory. But remember, do not tell the laird where Bowie is being held until he has paid in full."

"Aye," Thomas replied, eagerly nodding his flaxen head. "We will accept payment. Then we'll ride to the next village and hire a messenger to tell the laird where he can find his prize."

Nathan nodded in approval. "Be careful. Trust no one."

When Thomas and William had seized Bowie by the arms and began dragging him out into the street, Nathan turned to Caleb. "I'm ready for another ale."

Caleb frowned. "My guess is that ye've had too many cups as it is."

Nathan flashed a smile, clamping his hand on Caleb's shoulder. "As usual, my friend, ye've guessed wrong."

Caleb sat down across from him and raked a hand through his long, dark hair. "Ye should have waited."

Nathan waved his hand to show his lack of concern. "I did what I had to. I wasn't going to risk losing a purse like what Laird Cumming is willing to pay for Bowie."

"No amount of coin is worth dying for. Anyway, we've amassed enough wealth to live like kings for the rest of our days." Caleb set his sword on the table, and moved to sit down, but then his eyes flashed wide. "Do ye have some kind of death wish? Ye didn't even have yer sword," he said accusingly, picking up Nathan's blade where he had left it on the bench. "I thought that he disarmed ye."

Nathan felt a soft body press against his. He shifted in his seat and met warm eyes. The serving wench had returned, but this time, she brought two other lasses with her. "I was handling him," Nathan said absently as he allowed the women to settle on the benches. Straightaway, two nestled next to him and the other turned her attention to Caleb.

Caleb shook his head, seemingly unaware of the pretty dark-eyed lass nuzzling up close to him. "Ye may not care whether ye live or die, but some of us would prefer that ye lived."

"What are ye going on about? Ye worry too much," Nathan said before taking a long draught of ale. Then he raised his tankard. "Come, let us celebrate."

Caleb lifted his shoulders. "But what are we to celebrate? Yer near demise."

Nathan scoffed. "I had him bested."

"Ye take too many risks. When will it be enough?"

Nathan shrugged. "Only fools are satisfied," he drawled before downing the last of his ale.

Then he felt the pull of someone's gaze. He looked across the room and once again locked eyes with the lady who had arrived just before Bowie. Instantly, she shifted her gaze away from his, her attention now, at least in appearance, on the other corner of the room. But the slight pinking of her cheeks made him believe she was embarrassed for having been caught staring at him. The sight of her hair shimmering in the candlelight and the haughty angle of her chin renewed his interest.

Everything about her bespoke of restraint, from her straight back to her hands folded demurely in her lap, to her expressionless beauty. He continued to stare at her profile, wondering, once again, who she was and why a lady would come into The Devil's Bridge dressed as a commoner.

Then, to his surprise, she slowly shifted her gaze back to his, but this time, she did not look away. Her keen eyes and temptingly full lips were framed by a perfect oval face. He raised his tankard in greeting, but the maid on his left noticed the direction of his attention and cupped his cheek to redirect his gaze at her.

"I will do anything for ye, Nathan. Whatever yer heart desires."

Not to be outdone, the maid on his right boldly stroked her hand under his plaid. "As will I."

He kissed each woman in turn, slowly, tenderly. Then he leaned his head back against the wall and closed his eyes, inviting the numbness of drink to dull his thoughts while the distraction of the nameless, faceless women with roaming hands and soft lips made him forget it all—the highborn beauty in the corner, the look of innocent hope in Bowie's gaze, the truth of Caleb's warning, and the demons that never gave his soul reprieve.

# Chapter Three

E lora's heart had pounded while she watched the two men fight, believing for certain that the man who had attacked the giant was going to meet a quick death. After all, not only was he significantly smaller but he had also been unarmed.

She gazed over at the thief-taker who had returned to his table in the corner opposite her own. His appearance was striking. He had black hair, compelling deep-set eyes, and a strong jaw shadowed by rakish stubble. She watched as one of the serving maids leaned over the table seductively while setting another ale in front of him. His generous lips curved, lifting on one side in a sexy sideways smile that, to her own surprise, made Elora's breath catch.

Apparently, like every other woman in the room vying for his attention, she was not unaffected by his startling appeal.

In fact, she could hardly tear her gaze away from the lustful display taking place before her very eyes. The two women flanking his sides were beautiful despite their painted faces and common dress. Each freely explored his body while he drank his ale.

What piqued her curiosity was that he neither truly engaged

their advances nor did he push them away—as if it mattered not whether they stayed or gave their affection to someone else. His manner was careless, in the way he drank and passively allowed the women the use of his body.

She sucked in a sharp breath when he suddenly looked up and they locked eyes. Her face burned. Her heart raced, keeping her from meeting his gaze. The feeling unnerved her to her core. Her composure seldom wavered. Even when she was terrified, she was able to hide her fear from the world.

She scanned the tavern, pretending to be too occupied to notice the thief-taker's scrutiny. At length, her heart quieted, and she felt confident that she was once again the master of her emotions. Still feeling his gaze, she turned in his direction. They locked eyes, once again, and this time she held his gaze while she judged what sort of man he truly was.

One thing she knew for certain...He was fearless.

Attacking the armed criminal he had called Bowie with naught but his fists and lesser brawn certainly supported her belief, but it was not why she had made this assessment of his character.

It was in his eyes.

There was something distant in his gaze, even though his stare seemed to penetrate her very soul. It was as if he was not wholly there, as if he was someplace else, or even nowhere else. He raised his glass to her. She dipped her head slightly in greeting, but one of the women at his side scowled at her before forcing his gaze to meet hers.

A sweet, reassuring smile curved his lips as he cupped the woman's cheek and kissed her with the tenderness of an attentive lover. When he drew away, the woman's face held an almost reverent glow as if she had been anointed rather than simply appeased. He then turned and showed the other woman the same fleeting devotion. When both women renewed their impassioned advances, he took another long draught of ale before leaning his head back against the wall. Then he closed his eyes.

Elora knew at that moment that she, along with everything and everyone else, had been dismissed from his mind.

Meanwhile, he had only just begun to take root in her own thoughts.

She leaned close to Declan. "Speak with the barkeep. Find out everything ye can about that man," she said, looking pointedly at the dark-haired stranger.

"Aye, my lady," Declan replied. Then he stood and crossed to the bar while she continued to study the corner table opposite her own.

Elora watched fascinated by the fervor of the lusty women's actions and, in contrast, his passive response. Certainly, drink was to blame for his sluggish movements, but she was certain there was more to his disinterest.

A peal of feminine laughter drew her gaze to his companion who was also fine to look upon with dark hair and broad shoulders. In contrast, he had barely touched his cup and was giving his full attention to the young woman at his side. He whispered something in her ear, making her blush. Clearly, he could take what he wanted, but instead, he wooed her unnecessarily. In fact, Elora did not doubt that the brunette would welcome the gorgeous man freely into her arms, her bed, and her heart.

"My lady," Declan said, drawing her gaze. He slid back onto the bench across from her. "His name is Nathan Campbell. His companion is called Caleb, but no one can tell me his surname.

Nathan and his companions pass through here from time to time. They are thief-takers, as I'm sure ye've guessed, and apparently rather successful ones at that."

Elora looked over at Nathan, whose head was still back and his eyes closed.

"Is he of the southern Campbells?" she asked brightly, her mind fixed on the clan's great size and wealth.

"Nay, he hails from the north and is the chieftain's third son, although he is not in the laird's favor."

Her eyes widened. The laird's third son—his connections were better than she had dared hope. She chewed her bottom lip while she continued to study him. Despite her outer calm, her heart raced. He met her minimal requirements…He was a thief-taker, which meant he could be bought. Judging by his indulgent nature and recklessness, he was not overly concerned with his mortal soul, and he was a chieftain's son.

She turned to her guard. "I have made my choice." She nodded in Nathan's direction. "He's the one."

"The thief-taker? Nay, my lady! They're no better than criminals."

Ignoring Declan's protests, she continued. "I must speak with him, but not here. There are too many ears. Arrange for a room upstairs. Then ask him to come to me."

After Declan begrudgingly left to speak to the barkeep, Elora looked across the room. Nathan was still leaning against the wall with his eyes closed. She smiled, thinking that if he only knew what she was about to ask him, he would sober right up.

"To us," she said quietly and lifted her tankard to toast the man who she was certain could save her from a life of emptiness and misery.

# Chapter Four

"Nathan."

Nathan slowly opened his eyes and turned his head to meet the gaze of the wench on his left.

"Come upstairs. Ye don't need to pay." Her hand splayed wide against his chest. "I want ye in my bed."

"Maisie, I spotted him first," the barmaid sitting on his right snapped.

"Ye had him the last time he came through town. Tonight, he's mine."

Nathan peered into his tankard. "Empty," he mumbled to himself before he stood.

"Sit back down," both lassies said together.

He brushed past the one called Maisie and started toward the bar, when a man with hard, angry eyes suddenly appeared in front of him. Nathan blinked and cleared his thoughts, forcing his senses to sharpen.

"What do ye want?" he snapped. An instant later, Caleb appeared at his side.

"What's going on?" Caleb interjected.

"I do not ken." Nathan crossed his arms over his chest. "He hasn't said."

"Well, get on with it," Caleb demanded of the stranger.

Hands clenched at his sides, the man answered, "I need to speak with ye. 'Tis a business matter. I have a room upstairs."

With a slight shake of his head, Nathan brushed past the man.

"Find me on the morrow if ye wish to speak," he heard Caleb say.

"It must be now," the man replied. "Wait!"

Nathan stopped and slowly turned back. It was then that he recognized the man as the lady's guard. He jerked around and looked toward the corner table, but she was gone. Turning back to her guard, he said, knowingly, "'Tis she who wishes to see me."

The man nodded. "Will ye join her upstairs?"

Now, it all made sense.

The lady had come to the Devil's Bridge to find a mate for the night. She must be one of those pitiable creatures who had been forced to marry a much older man who couldn't possibly satisfy the hungers of the flesh. After all, she had given him a look of open appraisal. Clearly, she had chosen him to be her lover for the night. A smile curved his lips as he remembered how she had dusted off the bench before she sat. Mayhap beneath her rigid discipline beat a passionate heart.

Intrigued, he said, "Lead on."

He followed the guard toward the stairs, then noticed Caleb was trailing just behind. "She requested my company. If she wanted two men to fill her bed, I think she would have made that explicit."

A smile played at Caleb's lips. "Ye and I both know she is not what she seems, nor have we established anything explicit about her request other than wishing to see ye in private. Ye're not without enemies. When we are certain of her intentions, then I will leave ye to it."

"Suit yerself," Nathan shrugged before continuing after the guard.

They followed him upstairs. He knocked on a door.

"Enter," came a feminine reply from inside.

The guard swung the door wide, and the lady rose from her seat on a rough-hewn chair positioned next to a crackling brazier. Despite her simple, homespun garments, she was as regal as a queen.

A smile curved his lips. "My lady," he said, dipping his head to her.

The slight widening of her eyes revealed that he had surprised her.

"Ye're no common lass and I'm no fool."

"Good," she replied. "My needs cannot be satisfied by a fool."

He drew closer. "Then I am here to satisfy yer needs."

"Indeed," she said. "Why else would I have asked ye to join me?"

He looked pointedly at Caleb and the guard who were both standing near the door. "I believe we shall need some privacy."

She shook her head and came forward. "I see no need for that. Come in, gentlemen and close the door."

He cocked a brow at her. Never would he have guessed that she would have such wanton tastes. He swept his cloak off his shoulders and laid it on the back of the chair. "Shall we begin?"

"Indeed."

He crossed the room and stood in front of her, but she stiffly retreated back several steps.

He smiled and seized her waist, pulling her close. "Are we to play cat and mouse?" he asked, his voice husky.

"How dare ye?" she cried, pushing him away.

"Take yer hands off her!"

The familiar sound of a blade leaving its sheath rent the air, quickly followed by another.

Nathan whirled around. The guard brandished his sword at Nathan, a look of fury twisting his features while Caleb's sword was pointed at the guard.

"What are ye playing at?" Nathan growled, turning to face the woman.

"Me?" she scoffed. "'Tis ye who are in the wrong."

"There is usually only one reason a woman invites a man to her room."

With a haughty tilt of her chin, she gave him a sharp look, her delicate features showing her displeasure. "I have asked ye here so that we might converse in private."

He grabbed his cloak. "Conversation is the last thing I want right now."

"Ye will not speak so to her," the guard snapped again.

"Watch yer temper," Caleb said in reply, his tone holding an unmistakable warning.

"Insufferable men," the lady blurted. "Declan, put down yer sword."

"But, my lady," he began.

"Do as I've ordered!"

Without further hesitation, the guard complied.

Then she turned to Caleb. "Do the same."

Caleb, too, lowered his sword.

"Now, sit down," she commanded Nathan.

He considered antagonizing her further, but he was suddenly curious enough to know why she had arranged for their meeting. Taking a seat, he looked at her expectantly. "I'm listening."

"I am Lady Elora Brodie. My father passed away three months ago. At the time, he had been in negotiations with our neighbor, Laird Mackintosh, for my hand. A contract was never signed. Still, the laird pressures me to continue with the arrangements."

"And what does this have to do with me?"

"I have no intention of marrying him, but if I simply refuse, I risk offending him, which would surely lead to a feud."

"Again, I must ask what this has to do with me?"

"The only way I can see to avoid this marriage without violence is to make my own contract, and I have chosen ye to be my betrothed."

Nathan stiffened. Was this cold, highborn woman proposing marriage to him? He must have had more to drink than he thought. Standing, he said, "I will take my leave now." Then he turned and headed toward the door.

"I will pay ye handsomely," she called after him, but he did not stop to acknowledge her words.

Once in the hallway, Caleb chuckled. "For a moment, I was worried ye were going to accept her ladyship's offer."

Nathan cocked a brow at Caleb. "Now, why would ye imagine I would saddle myself with an uptight noblewoman?"

Caleb shrugged. "Because…ye would be laird of a wealthy clan."

Nathan stopped in his tracks. "Ye're right. I must be drunk." He turned around.

"Where are ye going?" Caleb called after him.

"I'm going to saddle myself with an uptight noblewoman." Nathan marched back to her room and threw open the door.

Elora swung around, her eyes wide.

"I will marry ye."

She crossed her arms over her chest and looked at him

pointedly. "Ye did not listen to me. Ye will be my betrothed. I said nothing about marriage."

Nathan canted his head to one side. "A betrothal and marriage are one in the same," he explained.

"Allow me to be explicit," she began. "We will be formally betrothed. We will speak vows sanctioned by a priest, but I promise ye now, we will never wed."

"'Tis blasphemous," Nathan pointed out.

"Having observed yer actions this evening, I took a chance that ye wouldn't be overly concerned about such matters."

"I'm not, but how is it that ye're able to make the same claim?"

Somehow, she tilted her chin even higher. "My soul is not yer concern. These are my terms. Ye will journey with me to my home where we will be promised to each other. This will allow me the time I need to devise a more permanent solution to my problem, after which, our contract will be annulled and ye will be free to leave with a handsome purse for yer effort. If ye accept, we leave at daybreak."

"So soon?"

"Laird Mackintosh's visit to Castle Bròn is imminent. Do ye have any other questions?"

"Why the pretense of marriage? Ye're a lady of wealth and beauty. Why do ye not arrange a proper union, mayhap even an alliance that will strengthen yer clan."

"I will never wed," she answered with finality.

"Never?" he repeated incredulously.

She nodded. "Ye heard my words."

"Who will lead yer people?"

Her eyes flashed with defiance, but her tone remained even when she spoke. "I will."

She certainly was not lacking in gumption, and he had to

admire the sheer boldness of her plan, defying custom and law—both man's and God's.

A smile curved his lips. "Ye may even be more reckless than me."

Her eyes narrowed on him, and she took a step forward. "Recklessness is akin to carelessness. I'm never careless."

He was growing increasingly intrigued by Lady Elora Brodie. "Do ye accept my terms?"

He nodded. "I do."

"Fine," she replied, her voice clipped. "Meet me out front on the morrow. Do not be late."

"Fine," Nathan responded, mirroring her tone.

He continued to study her. She withstood his scrutiny for several moments with her same unwavering calm before saying, "Ye may go."

He smiled at her frankness. "Until the morrow," he said and dipped his head in farewell before he turned and left the room with Caleb following close behind.

"She is a courageous woman," Nathan said, once they were in the hallway.

"Terrified is a more apt description, although most would not have detected her fear," Caleb pointed out.

"If she wasn't afraid, she would have no reason for courage," Nathan shot back. "Her desperation is blinding her to the holes in her plan, but fortunately, for me, I can see everyone."

Caleb cocked a brow at him. "Are ye truly considering actual marriage?"

"Nay," he answered. "I'm done considering the matter. I've no doubt that she will be my wife, and I will be Laird of Clan Brodie."

"And then, what?" Caleb asked. "What will that satisfy?"

Nathan stopped and looked him dead on. "Remember, only fools are satisfied."

They headed back downstairs to their table much to the delight of the three maids who cheered upon their return, but he no longer had room in his mind for them. He looked up at the ceiling, realizing that the woman now dominating his thoughts was in a room directly overhead. At that moment, he laughed outright, imagining her standing in naught but her kirtle, wrinkling her nose in disgust while she eyed the tavern's worn, straw mattress.

"To us," he said quietly, raising his tankard to the ceiling, toasting the woman who would make him laird, but then he faltered, setting his cup back down without taking a sip. The idea of greater wealth and power had done nothing to stir his soul. He laid his head back and closed his eyes and welcomed the numbness to once again overtake his thoughts.

# Chapter Five

Elora awoke to the sounds of squawking seagulls, sailors calling out orders, and the mighty din of shipbuilders. She sat up and crossed to the window and opened the shutters, letting the crisp sea air lift her unbound hair. It was the hour before daybreak. The sky overhead was as black as pitch. But as her gaze traveled across the heavens, the sky lightened to the deepest blue, gradually becoming lighter still until it collided with the horizon beyond the Water of Leith where the North Sea touched the sky in a gleaming strip of fiery orange.

Those lonely hearts she had witnessed the night before—hearts filled with yearning, haunting regret, and the agony of loss now slept while the courageous had arisen to face the dawn. A slow smile spread across her face as her heart warmed to Edinburgh's bustling harbor. The earliest light of a new day revealed the waterside's charm and vitality.

Sailors, no longer idle or drunk, loaded crates onto skiffs bound for fishing vessels and merchant cogs that were anchored in deeper waters. She admired their nimble, swaying movements, which matched the rhythm of the waves like a dance only seafarers could know.

She closed her eyes and imagined herself among their number, readying to set sail. In that moment, she could feel the pull of the sea and the call of the ships. It was majestic and mournful. Joyful, yet imbued with heartbreaking sorrow. She leaned out beyond the casement, closed her eyes, and let her unbound hair catch the breeze. A shiver of excitement shot up her spine as sensation surrounded her—the sound of the waves, the salty air, the fiery horizon a breath away from releasing the fullness of day. Smiling, she opened her eyes just in time to see the sun crest beyond the confines of its blanketed retreat.

But as it emerged, so, too, did Lady Brodie. With a disciplined heart, she shrugged off the pang of sadness that cut through her soul and stood straight.

There wasn't room for sunrises or glittering waves in her world.

Turning away from the window and the fatal allure of the sea, she began taming her wild curls into two thick plaits.

Her own purpose came to the fore of her thoughts. Not unlike the sailors and business owners readying their shops, she, too, had a schedule to keep.

After donning her borrowed tunic and cloak, she stood in front of the door. Straightening her back, she took a deep breath, gave a determined tilt to her chin, and swung the door wide.

"Good morrow," she said to Declan who she was not surprised to find waiting for her in the hallway.

He dipped his head to her. "Good morrow, Elora. The horses are packed and ready."

"Good," she replied and took his offered arm.

Together, they made their way downstairs. She wrinkled her nose against the smell of stale beer and waste. The revelers from the previous night had departed, except for one young man curled up beneath a table.

"New to his cups, I'd wager," Declan said, gesturing to the sleeping lad.

Elora lifted her skirt as she carefully picked her way around splatters of pottage, puddles of ale and what she wanted to believe was ale. Tankards and bowls of half-eaten pottage still littered the tables.

She hastened toward the door. Stepping out into the morning light, she expelled a sigh of relief when she saw her white mare.

"Rosie," she whispered, allowing her lips to hint at a smile while she stroked the horse's muzzle affectionately. Then she turned to Declan and said, "I hope never to see the inside of that place again."

Declan nodded in agreement. "I will be happy to leave the city behind altogether."

"As will I. We will not linger," she assured him. "As soon as Nathan joins us, we will depart." Elora looked around expectantly. "I did tell him daybreak, did I not?"

"Aye, ye did," Declan confirmed.

She smoothed her hands over her tunic. "I'm certain his arrival is imminent. Please help me mount, so that we may ride out straightaway."

Declan leaned down and interlaced his fingers. Elora placed her slippered foot in his hand, gripped the saddle horn, and with a bounce and Declan's boost, she settled herself on Rosie's back. Then she smoothed her tunic and situated her cloak.

"Ready," she said to her guard.

He mounted his horse. "As am I."

Nodding her approval, she turned her attention to The Devil's Bridge from which she was certain her newly hired help would soon exit.

After staring at the door for some time, tension crept up her spine, laying claim to her shoulders. Still, she maintained her calm.

With a look of thinly veiled hope, Declan asked, "Shall we just leave?"

"Please do not start that again." Taking a deep breath to keep her frustration at bay, she shifted her focus away from the tavern.

The sun had emerged fully, banishing any lingering darkness, and casting myriad colors across the sea and sky. Fishmongers were preparing their wagons to take to market. Skiffs of varying sizes were skidding away on the rippling waves in radiant shades of rose and gold. Tearing her gaze from the sea, she shifted in her saddle, her attention drawn by a new sound. Looking behind her, she spied the blacksmith throwing open the gates to his shop. He was broadly built with massive shoulders. Further down the road, she saw a wizened old man with a hunched back slowly swinging open the door to the apothecary. Assisting him was the scrubby young lad she had seen the night before selling hot pig feet.

Shielding her eyes, she gazed at the sun. It crawled higher and higher. "'Tis past *Lauds*," she observed tensely.

"Indeed," Declan agreed. "We should leave now while the weather is still in our favor."

Elora turned and followed his gaze to the west. Heavy clouds were beginning to gather in loose clusters. Her nostrils flared.

Nathan's delay was threatening her well-planned trip home.

Echoing her thoughts, Declan continued his attempts to persuade her to leave. "We need to reach Grant territory this day. It would be unwise to solicit Laird Grant's hospitality after nightfall."

She waved away his concern. "Laird Grant is a trusted ally. There is nothing he would deny me...including his own son," she said under her breath.

The aged leader of Clan Grant had lost his wife and only child to fever when Elora was an infant. Broken hearted, he did not marry again for many years. Eventually, he chose a lass from among his clan and made her his bride. Together, they had a son, William, who was a gentle, thoughtful lad with only ten and three years.

When Elora had recently confided to Laird Grant that the Mackintosh was pressuring her to marry, Laird Grant proposed that she marry his young son instead. Of course, the union would be in name only until William was of age, but at one and twenty, Elora had no wish to bind herself to a child.

More importantly, she had no wish to bind herself to anyone.

Once again, she turned and watched The Devil's Bridge expectantly.

"Listen, my lady," Declan exclaimed.

Above the din of the harbor, she heard a distant bell toll the hour of *Prime*. A flash of anger coursed through her. Her hands squeezed her reins.

"My lady, I will go rouse him," Declan offered. But just at that moment the tavern door opened, and Nathan stepped out, shielding his eyes from the light of the new day.

"Good morrow," he called when he saw her.

She did not spare him a smile but simply dipped her head in greeting. "Mount yer horse and let's ride. Ye've delayed me long enough."

With a smile playing at his lips, he walked toward her. "Is she always this demanding first thing in the morning?" he said off-handedly to Declan.

Declan gave Nathan a look of warning. "Do not speak ill of my lady."

Nathan's smile widened, and he bowed with exaggerated gallantry. Then he straightened and crossed to Rosie's side and began slowly stroking her white mane. When he looked up and met Elora's gaze, her pulse quickened. She hadn't forgotten how fine he was to look upon, with his dark tousled curls, but what she hadn't realized yesterday was that his eyes were not blue—they were silver. A gentle smile curled his lips. "I was only intending to be playful as a husband might with his wife. I'm simply becoming accustomed to my new role."

His insinuation was a welcomed distraction from his smile. "Yer new *temporary* role," she reminded him. "As my betrothed, never my husband."

"On that point, ye've been very clear," he said softly. Then he turned his back to her and started to walk away.

"Where are ye going?"

"I'm meeting Caleb at the livery to fetch our horses," he called back.

Stifling an unladylike screech, she squeezed the reins harder, her knuckles whitening from the strain and glanced over at Declan who was giving her a pointed look.

"I ken, Declan. Ye disapprove of him."

"And ye do not?"

"Of course, I do not approve of him. He is a thief-taker and a renegade, but, for the last time, I did not come here to choose my rightful husband. I came here to find a man willing to flout the law, both God's and man's."

Declan pressed his lips together in a grim line, but he made no further comment.

At length, Nathan and Caleb trotted toward them on sinewy,

black stallions.

With a cool nod of her head, she called. "Let us ride!"

"Are ye certain about that?"

Reins lifted, ready to gently snap, she paused and met Nathan's silver gaze. "I am. In fact, I've been certain. Naught has changed since last night when ye agreed to my terms, naught except the hour of our departure," she said pointedly. "If ye recall, my instructions were to leave at daybreak."

His gaze shifted to the harbor. "To the east, I yet see the dawn reflected on the water. Daybreak is still upon us. If ye had an hour in mind, ye should have been more specific."

She bristled at his scolding, but before she could issue a stern rebuttal, he looked away from the sea, toward distant, rolling moorland and said, "To the west, I see angry clouds preparing to be heard. 'Tis going to storm...hard. Ye might wish to delay our journey a day or two."

She shook her head. "I have also noted the gathering rain clouds, but we cannot delay another moment. I must return at once to Castle Bròn." Without waiting for his reply, she nudged Rosie with her heels and set out in the lead.

Once they cleared the city gates, she clicked her tongue and Rosie surged ahead at a quick trot. Soon, Edinburgh faded in the distance. Even the city's towering stronghold was just a blur on the horizon.

Declan rode at her side while Nathan and Caleb followed closely behind. She kept her gaze forward, her back straight in the saddle, her outer calm unwavering, all the while wishing with her whole heart that a magic wind could lift them high and carry them home.

The sun continued to climb. She raised her face to the light and closed her eyes.

"Spring is upon us," Declan said, drawing her gaze.

"Aye," she nodded, sparing her loyal servant a rare smile. "I feel spring's promise," she said, upturning her face once more to the sun.

But then shadow overcame the light, stealing the sun's warmth. She opened her eyes. The dark clouds were spreading quickly, pulling together to blanket the blue sky.

"If we turned back now, we might be able to beat the storm back to Edinburgh."

She stiffened in her seat, hearing Nathan's voice. He moved his horse alongside hers. She turned and met his gaze. She was far from being one of the many lusty women at The Devil's Bridge, throwing themselves at him. Still, she had to admit that she was not unaffected by his chiseled jaw, deep-set eyes, and full mouth. She cleared her throat. "It rained hard on our journey here."

"Nothing more than a drizzle when compared to what will soon be unleashed upon our heads."

She looked him straight on. "I have no intention of turning back."

He gave her an assessing look before he shrugged his shoulders. "I only wanted to save yer ladyship from becoming cold and sodden."

She did not look forward to the prospect of traveling in the midst of a storm either, but no amount of rain could be a greater threat than the one looming ahead. She needed to return home and make her betrothal official to the wickedly handsome, irritating, and interfering man at her side, before Laird Mackintosh arrived at Castle Bròn.

"I'm not a delicate flower that might wilt in a wee bit of rain," she said simply. Then she drove her heel into Rosie's flank to sprint ahead, putting herself, once again, in the lead.

Tension filled her shoulders as she rode. Her temporary betrothed clearly wanted to take command, but unlike most of her sex, she was neither submissive nor demur. The steward of Bròn was loyal to her as was Declan. Her people believed in her and honored her with their fealty. She straightened her back. What did it matter what Nathan sought or believed? He would soon come to realize that she was not a woman with which to be trifled.

The first drops of rain fell, cool and crisp, alighting on her brow and hands with a gentle pitter patter. But soon the crisp droplets gave way to a steady assault. It was not long until she was wet through to her skin. Still, she did not soften her back or shield her face from the pelting rain. Clenching her teeth to keep them from chattering, she refused to reveal her true discomfort. Weakness was something men could sense, and she would not give Nathan the satisfaction of knowing how much she wished the sun yet favored their journey.

Soon, rolling moorland revealed a stretch of wood in the distance, for which she was grateful. At least the trees would offer some coverage from the downpour.

"We should stay our course and go around the wood," Nathan said, once more pulling his horse beside her.

She shook her head. "We cut through the forest."

"But a river passes through the easterly part of that wood."

She kept her gaze straight ahead. "I am aware of that."

"'Tis March. The river floods this time of year. We must think of the horses."

She dismissed his concerns with a wave of her hand. "We took this same road not two days ago and had no trouble crossing the river."

His wet, black curls clung to his face, framing his silver eyes. He held his hand out, letting the rain splatter his palm. "Ye must account for these last days of hard rain. The westerly road around the wood will take longer, but it will be less tiring to the horses."

She shook her head. "We're going to sleep tonight under the protection of Clan Grant. Already our arrival will be later than I planned because of our delayed departure," she said, allowing displeasure to enter her tone. "Rosie is strong, and ye and Caleb ride sturdy beasts. I'm certain we'll be able to cross the river somewhere."

"That I do not doubt, but the effort will be taxing."

Caleb brought his horse in line with Nathan's. His dark head was covered by the hood of his cloak. "We're not far from Stewart territory. They've a hunting lodge on the edge of their land. We are well known to Laird Stewart. He'll not object to us seeking shelter from the storm."

Her eyes widened. "A hunting lodge!" She paused for a moment, reclaiming her usual calm. "Why bother?" she scoffed, "when we can lay our heads on the sodden ground."

A slight smile upturned Nathan's lips. "Had I known ye would be so amendable to sleeping out of doors, it would have been my first suggestion."

She lifted her chin stubbornly. "I would like to remind ye that I have hired ye and not the other way around. I am leading our party. It should be evident to ye that I am not an animal. I do not sleep out of doors. I also would appreciate if in the future, ye keep yer suggestions to yerself. We will reach Grant territory this day. On this point, I am unwavering."

Nathan gave her an assessing look before quietly saying, "Lead on, my lady."

She straightened her back, refusing to admit her discomfort, and nudged Rosie forward. The way through the wood was slow going. Fallen tree limbs littered the path, which was slick with mud. The rain became more intense, and soon she heard the distant rush of the river. They had yet to stop and rest their mounts, and already Rosie's breathing was becoming labored.

She leaned over in her saddle and stroked her hot neck. "Ye can do this," she whispered encouragingly. Squeezing the reins in her hands to cease her trembling, she prayed that she had not been hasty in her judgment.

"Blast," she muttered under her breath. The river roared like thunder. As she approached the swiftly moving current, her horse's hooves began to sink in the mud.

Declan drew up beside her. "Fear not, my lady. We will find a safe place to cross. I have crossed many a river in my day."

"Aye, but I have not," she admitted quietly. She glanced at Nathan who was watching her intently from several feet away. Seldom away from Bròn, she was unaccustomed to travel. She realized, in that moment, that her lack of experience had informed a foolish choice.

As if sensing her hesitation, Nathan drew close. Without a word he dismounted and took the reins from her hands. With his horse and Rosie in tow, he stepped forward, his tall leather brogues sinking in the mud. A moment later Declan and Caleb did the same, leading their horses.

"Stop, Nathan. Declan," she called to her guard. "Help me down. I will lead Rosie."

Nathan glanced back at her, a gentle smile playing at his lips. "I'd like to see ye navigate these waters in yer tunic, unless ye intend to hitch it above yer knees."

Her pulse raced as she felt herself losing control over the

situation, but the idea of revealing the better part of her legs to her companions silenced her protests. She had no choice but to allow Nathan to take the reins.

At first, the horses snorted and resisted entering the water. To her relief, Nathan did not force them. Instead, he walked further along the shore.

"Ye're letting them choose where to cross," she observed.

He nodded and in a quiet voice said, "The horses will find the surest footing themselves."

Finally, Nathan's stallion began to wade deeper into the river, but Rosie hesitated. Nathan turned and pressed his cheek to hers. "'Tis all right, lass," Elora heard him croon, his voice tender. He clicked his tongue and continued to encourage her, until, at last, she took her first tentative steps into deeper waters. Behind her, Declan and Caleb followed, each leading their horses.

When they reached the other side, apprehension washed over Elora. Rosie hung her head low, her white mane dragging the ground. "'Tis all right, lass."

Nathan turned to face her.

"We must rest the horses," she said quickly before he could, seizing the moment to reestablish her authority.

But to her surprise, he shook his head. "Nay, we make camp."

She stiffened. "What? *Vespers* must yet be hours away."

"We make camp," he said again.

"Nay, I will not sleep on the ground."

"My lady," Declan began, rubbing the back of his neck awkwardly. "Nathan is right. We'll never make it to Grant land. Even Stewart territory is beyond the reach of our horses now. If we carry on, we'll end up having to make camp on the open moors. At least here we will be under the cover of the trees."

She shook her head. "For all we know, the storm may be subsiding." Just then a roar of thunder rumbled in the distance and the rain came down all the harder, mocking her hopeful prediction.

Without a word, Nathan mounted his horse. Once again, he grasped Rosie's reins and started to lead them off the forest path, deeper into the thicket.

"I can manage her myself," Elora snapped, feeling her temper rise. She pressed her lips together, regretting her uncharacteristic outburst. Still, she withstood Nathan's probing gaze.

At length, he handed back her reins. Then he continued forward. She sat still for a moment, searching her mind for some way to gain back the upper hand.

"My lady, are ye all right?" Declan asked behind her.

"I'm fine," she lied.

Tension filling her shoulders, she nudged her horse forward, knowing there was nothing she could do but follow Nathan's lead.

# Chapter Six

The fierce rain carved rivulets into the sodden muddy earth and pelted tree limbs and spring's first leaves. The din was deafening. Her heart quickened every time her mind returned to the very reason she had set out on what she now was beginning to fear was a hopeless quest. What if the Mackintosh arrived at Castle Bròn before she did? Unless she had another marriage contract blessed and signed before he reached their front gate, she could only refuse his advances at risk to her people.

It came as no surprise when her father had announced his choice for her husband. Laird Mackintosh mirrored the deceased chieftain of Clan Brodie in every way. He was cruel and ambitious to the point of blindness. He would only bring hardship to her people.

She stiffened in her seat when Nathan suddenly turned and glanced back at her, his brow drawn. "Are ye all right?" he called over the din.

Nay! She wanted to shout. She was freezing, wet to the bone, frustrated, not to mention worried, but she was not going to tell him the truth. A curt nod of her head was her only reply.

He turned back around and rode on. Despite the cold and

drenching rain, he was relaxed in the saddle. She watched him sway side to side in a gentle rhythm, matching the stomping of his stallion's hooves. Her gaze traced his broad, powerful shoulders and well-muscled legs as he rode.

"My lady, I am going to pass ye on yer right," Declan shouted from behind.

He did as he had warned and pulled his horse alongside Nathan's. She watched with unease while her guard conferred with their new leader. What they were discussing, she could not say, which only heightened her frustration. But Nathan was nodding, listening intently to Declan. In response, he gestured further up the path. Declan appeared to nod, seemingly in agreement. Then he rode ahead, no doubt to carry out Nathan's bidding while Nathan fell back, bringing his horse alongside Rosie.

"There is a clearing up ahead that will have to do for the night," he said.

She nodded but said nothing as she fought to keep herself from shivering in the cold.

As if he could read her thoughts, his black brows drew together, showing his concern. "It will be all right, my lady."

"Of course, it will," she said, grasping for her courage.

Sure enough, the trees thinned out and soon they rode into a glade free from underbrush but still canopied by tree boughs.

Straightaway, Nathan dismounted and crossed to her side. Without a word, he reached up and placed his hands at her waist.

Her eyes widened. "What are ye doing?"

One corner of his mouth lifted in a slight smile. "I'm helping ye down, my lady."

His silver eyes locked with hers. He lifted her off the saddle, then lowered her to the ground, achingly slow. Her heart pounded as his strong hands held her. When her feet touched down, his hands lingered at her waist, and she did not step away. His gaze held hers captive. Not for the first time, she glimpsed something in his eyes. She couldn't name what she saw. It wasn't lustful desire—she had experienced the wantonness of men enough at clan gatherings and had even caught the men of Brodie looking at her with desire. His gaze was intent but still somehow distant, even though he held her closer than any man had ever dared.

At length, she cleared her throat. His hands dropped away. She stepped back, her waist still burning from his touch.

"Nathan," she heard Caleb say, drawing his silver gaze away. She turned, and pretended to be occupied with soothing Rosie, when, in fact, she fought to catch her breath.

"My lady," Declan called. With relief, she turned her attention to her kinsman who had propped a saddle against a tree, and now stood with a blanket outstretched in his arms. "'Tis wet, but 'tis better than naught. Come and sit here while we ready camp."

She looked at Declan's makeshift chair and blanket with longing, but more immediate than her own comfort was her need to reclaim her authority. Turning to face the men, she set her hands on her hips, ready to take command, but then she faltered. She knew how to ask that the home fires be lit, but not how to light the fire herself. She knew how to organize dozens of servants to keep Bròn running smoothly, but she knew nothing of making camp.

Resigned to relinquish control, at least temporarily, she settled herself on the saddle.

Declan wrapped her in the blanket. "Thank ye," she said.

Then she watched as he turned and joined with the other men. Nathan easily took command, and to her surprise, she couldn't find fault in his plans or how he spoke to her kinsman. First, the men turned their attention to the horses, brushing away burs and dried mud from their coats and scraping their hooves clean. Next, they set to work cutting branches and whittling the wood down to the dry layers, which they piled on top of thin shavings. Soon, they had a small fire.

When, at last, the men were ready to rest, they circled around the wee dancing flames.

Elora reached her hands toward the heat. "Thank ye for yer hard work."

"Of course, my lady," Declan replied.

Caleb nodded in acknowledgment, his blue eyes kind.

"My pleasure," Nathan said. She shifted her gaze to meet his. His face was, once again, impassive.

She cleared her throat. "We've dried stag," she offered, and began to divide their remaining supply, but her hands, still aching from the cold, shook as she worked.

"Thank ye," Nathan said, accepting his portion, only he did not take the meat. Instead, he clasped her hands in his.

Her breath caught.

"Ye're so cold," he said softly.

She swallowed hard, pulling her hands free. "I'm fine," she said, looking away, confused by his gentle manner. Then she remembered that he had not always been a thief-taker. He had been born a chieftain's son and no doubt had the education and training befitting his station.

When the last of the meat had been eaten, Caleb stood and dipped his head to her. "I bid ye goodnight, my lady." He turned and crossed to the far side of the glade and wrapped the top folds of his plaid around his shoulders. Then he laid down with his back to the fire and to them.

Declan's brows drew together. "Did we do something that might have offended yer companion?"

Nathan shook his head. "Caleb prefers the quiet of his own company."

Declan's worry eased from his face. "That I understand. I often seek out the comfort of solitude, do I not, my lady?"

Elora smiled at her kinsman. "Indeed, ye do. I credit yer wisdom and patience to the many hours ye spend at prayer, alone in the kirk."

Always modest, Declan shook his head, waving away her praise.

"What of ye, Nathan?" she asked quietly.

He did not answer right away, which she was beginning to realize was his habit. Instead, he held her gaze. Tilting her chin higher, she forced herself not to look away or squirm beneath his scrutiny. At length, he answered, "The less I have to listen to my own thoughts the better." Then he raised his face to the rain and closed his eyes.

His answer both intrigued and saddened her, and for some inexplicable reason she wanted to reach over and take his hand in hers and...

"We should all rest," she blurted and stood, shrugging the blanket off her shoulders. Then she spread it out on the ground.

Declan helped her smooth out the wrinkles. "My lady," he began.

She looked up and met his gaze, surprised to see a hint of pink coloring his weathered cheeks.

"It occurs to me," he continued, "that if I turn my back to ye, I do not think it would be indecent, considering our circumstances, were you to lie close to me to keep warm."

Shivering, she nodded. "I believe ye're correct in yer thinking. Thank ye, Declan."

Nathan stood then and met her gaze. He closed the distance between them. "Will ye be all right?" His tone was husky. A tightness entered her chest. She was moved by the concern she heard in his voice, but then she glimpsed his devil's charm as the sideways smile curved one side of his lips. "I'll warm yer other side."

His sensual words reminded her that he was a rake, hired for a single purpose. She would not allow his occasional thoughtfulness to become a distraction. She shook her head. "I'm fine."

When she turned to walk away, he gently seized her arm. "Forgive my jest." He reached out and stroked the back of his fingers down her cheek. "Ye're like ice."

"I'm becoming quite accustomed to the cold," she lied, trying to keep her teeth from chattering.

He gave her a knowing look. "Should ye change yer mind, I will just be over there," he said, gesturing to the other side of the fire.

Shivering, she lay on the freezing, wet blanket. As promised, Declan turned his back to her. She sidled up next to him, pressing her back against his. Then she covered herself with her cloak. It was not long until she heard Declan's even breaths, signaling he had, despite the rain and cold, somehow fallen asleep. She knew, of course, that the head of her guard, who had one and forty years to his credit, was a seasoned warrior and had known worse nights than a rainstorm in a peaceful glade. She, on the other hand, had never slept out of doors, not to mention in the rain when spring had not yet fully laid claim to the land. Tears flooded her eyes. Unable to restrain herself any longer, her teeth chattered, and her body shook. She turned into Declan's back, huddling close and prayed for sleep to take her pain away.

But then she heard something stirring behind her. Her eyes flashed wide. An instant later, strong arms surrounded her, and she was pulled against a hard, warm body.

"Nay," she gasped, twisting to free herself.

"Hush," a deep voice crooned in her ear. "Pretend ye like the feel of my arms. It will be good practice since I will soon be yer betrothed."

She lay stiffly in Nathan's arms, her teeth chattering uncontrollably.

"Do not resist my help," he said, rocking her gently.

"Blast," she cursed and quickly turned into his embrace, burying her face in his neck. He crushed her against himself, and it did not occur to her to fight him again. She had never been held by a man. Under any other circumstances, she would have been furious, scandalized. But at that moment, she needn't pretend to enjoy Nathan's embrace as he had bidden her. His warmth surrounded her. His strength comforted her. She breathed deep his masculine scent. Slowly, her shivering ceased, and she eased her shoulders away from her ears. The tension fled her body. She melted into Nathan's warmth, savoring his heat. Softening her whole body, she wiggled as close to him as she could.

"My lady," he whispered, his voice hoarse. "Ye must hold still."

She pulled away a little. "I'm not shivering any longer."

"Aye, but ye're still moving."

"I do not mean to keep ye awake."

"Ye're awakening more than ye realize," he said, his voice

strained.

She blushed when she realized what he was trying to convey. He desired her.

What struck her to her core was that she was neither repelled nor offended.

In fact, she was breathless. Never had she known such intimacy before.

Now, she couldn't sleep but not for the cold. It was the heat of his body that kept her awake and the knowledge of his desire. She tried to turn her thoughts elsewhere—anywhere other than the feel of Nathan's hard, chiseled physique pressed against her racing heart. Still, no matter how she tried, she could not deny her response to his touch. Silently cursing herself, she fought for command over her emotions. Forcing her breathing to steady, she strengthened her resolve. She would not allow herself to be so easily tempted by a man, especially one who drank to oblivion and shared his bed with a different woman every night. It mattered not how good he smelled, or how strong his embrace, or how captivated she was by the secrets she glimpsed in his silver gaze.

His hand smoothed down her back. "Are ye warm now?"

She bit her bottom lip, choking back her honest response. Nay! She was hot! Painfully hot, and in places she never knew could ache.

"I'm fine," she said, relieved by the coolness of her tone.

"Sweet dreams," he murmured, nestling close. "I know mine will be."

"Good night," she answered stiffly, praying her dreams were sweet...sweet and proper and full of restraint.

# Chapter Seven

Girlish laughter echoed in Nathan's mind as he opened his eyes. Standing in the shadowy glade was a young lass with ten and four years. Bits of hay and grass clung to her black, unbound curls and green tunic. She smiled, her beautiful face warm and full of life.

"Come along, Nathan," she laughed. "Catch me if ye can!"

"Cait," he whispered, reaching out his hand.

The lass turned and started to run away from him.

"Come back," he whispered, but she faded away, becoming nothing more than mist and memory.

He closed his eyes against the vision as familiar as the ache that stole his breath. He clung to the woman in his arms, waiting for the pain to pass. The scent of her hair surrounded him. Her softness and the evenness of her sleeping breaths calmed him. Pressing a kiss to her brow, he closed his eyes and drifted back to sleep.

~ * ~

"Good morrow, Nathan."

Nathan stirred, slowly opening his eyes. Shadow still lingered, but birdsong ushered in the promise of morning. He lifted his head and smiled at Elora, her smooth hand at rest on his chest. "Good morrow, my lady."

She looked up at him expectantly. "Ye're holding me so tightly, 'tis a wonder I can still breathe."

Chuckling, he lay his head back on the ground. "Ye're warm, aren't ye?"

She cleared her throat. "As much as I appreciate yer…er…help, I would prefer if Declan did not know that I spent the night…" Her words trailed off.

"Lying in my arms," he finished for her.

"Precisely."

Nathan closed his eyes and for a moment, a breath, he held her tighter, drawing comfort from her embrace that reached soul-deep. Then, slowly, he loosened his arms. She pulled away and began to sit up, taking away the solace of her touch.

He forced his eyes to open and his legs to stand. Every breath and step he took pushed it all down, all his pain, deep down; until there was nothing.

"Let us wake the others," Elora said, drawing his gaze.

Her delicate features came into focus. The stern set had returned to her jaw. Her shoulders were pushed back, and her spine was as rigid as ever. He forced his lips into a smile. "Ye're eager to be off, I'd wager."

"We must leave straightaway." She turned and crossed to Declan's side. Crouching down, she gently shook the older warrior awake.

Nathan turned to find Caleb already standing. Nathan nodded in greeting before retreating deeper into the thicket to relieve himself. When he returned to the clearing, the others had already mounted their horses.

"We ride," Elora said, her tone and bearing, once again, that of a lady used to giving orders.

He mounted his horse. "Lead on."

Her blue eyes flashed wide for a moment as if she were surprised to find him so compliant. He dipped his head to her to further show his cooperation.

With a curt nod, she turned and set out in the lead.

He followed behind her, his gaze trailing over her shapely curves as she bounced in the saddle. He could still feel her body, soft and supple, in his arms, the way she'd clung to him, seeking his warmth, his comfort. He closed his eyes, remembering her sleek waist, the flare of her hips, and her thigh draped over his. Opening his eyes, he nudged his horse with his heel and started forward. A slight smile curved his lips as he watched her in the lead. She rode with rigid discipline, beautiful and statuesque. But now he couldn't help but wonder about the woman beneath her shield of polished stone.

When they reached the edge of the wood, early morning's light still clung to the land. The moors stretched out in front of them, rolling and shadowy all the way to the horizon where the sun burned ember-bright. Dark clouds, lined with pink and gold littered the sky.

Once on the open moors, Nathan quickened his pace, bringing his mount alongside Rosie. Elora looked his way for a moment and nodded her head in greeting, but she then shifted her gaze back to the path ahead.

"Do not fash yerself, my lady. We will reach Brodie land this day."

She turned then and met his gaze. "Reaching home does me little good, if Laird Mackintosh arrives before me."

He sat straighter in his saddle. "Then we'd best beat him

there."

Their eyes locked. "Yes, we must," she said firmly.

He smiled slightly and looked at the horizon. "The clouds fade into mist. The weather is on yer side." Then he turned back to face her. "Our horses are rested. Let us ride!"

A look of unshakable determination entered her eyes as she drove her heels into her horse's flanks. Then, they raced over the rolling hills like skiffs riding the great waves of the North Sea. The rush of air and the speed of their pace pulsed through Nathan, giving him a rare moment of feeling truly alive.

Stopping only to eat and water their horses, they pushed on through the morning. Finally, when the sun rose overhead, Elora reined in her horse and pointed toward a sprawling village and beyond that a castle strategically positioned on a hilltop with turreted towers at each corner.

Nathan brought his mount to a halt beside hers.

"Brodie Village and Castle Bròn," she said calmly, her face unreadable, but as always, her knuckles were white from her tight grip on the reins. He reached over and covered one of her hands with his. "'Tis all right to feel excited, my lady."

She jerked her hand away, giving him a curious look. "I know," she said simply. Then she snapped her reins and set out, once more, at a gallop.

Puzzled by her ever constant restraint, he gave chase after her with Declan and Caleb following just behind. Before too long, moorland gave way to fields, which busy cottars readied for the April planting. They stopped their labor when their lady came into view and cheered, calling her name. She dipped her head in greeting, her regal manner never faltering.

When they reached the village, people, young and old, men and women, raced to greet their lady as she rode by.

"Welcome home, my lady!"

"My lady, ye're home!"

"God bless Lady Elora!"

Upon their first meeting, he had pictured her as a haughty lady, selfish and demanding. Clearly, he had been wrong. The devotion of her people was a testimony of her character.

Leaving the village behind, Elora led the charge up the hill and through the gates of Castle Bròn, straight into the courtyard where a tall man with broad shoulders and long silver hair stood in the center, his arms crossed over his chest.

Elora drew to a halt next to him and slid to the ground. "Am I too late?"

"Nay, but we received a missive yesterday. Laird Mackintosh arrives this eventide."

"How long do we have?"

"A few hours at best."

Nathan swung down from his horse. The older man's eyes narrowed as he met Nathan's gaze.

"I suppose this is him," he said, his scowl deepening.

"Aye," Elora replied. "This is Nathan Campbell." Then she turned to Nathan. "This is my steward, Murray Brodie."

Nathan dipped his head in greeting, but the steward of Clan Brodie ignored him and turned to Elora. "Please reconsider, my lady."

"Do not waste time, Murray. We haven't a moment to spare." She seized Nathan's hand and started to pull him toward the castle steps.

Confused, Nathan asked, "I don't understand. Time for what? What's happening?"

Without a backward glance, she shook her head. "I'll explain later."

Passing through towering double doors, they entered the great hall of Castle Bròn.

"Elora," a feminine voice squealed. Then, in a flash of black curls, a young woman raced toward Elora and threw herself into her arms.

Nathan froze at the sight of the dark-haired lass, his heart lodged in his throat. Tension flooded his body. He closed his eyes. His nostrils flared as he took a deep breath. It was not the first time he had encountered a lass who resembled the one haunting his dreams…nor would it be the last. Steeling his heart, he watched their happy reunion.

"I've been so worried," the young woman cried. Tears streamed down her snow-white cheeks.

"'Tis all right now," he heard Elora say in a soothing voice. Then she pulled away. "Deep breath. We haven't time for tears."

Nodding, the lass swiped at her cheeks. "I ken," she said bravely. Then she looked past Elora at Nathan, and then beyond him to where Declan and Caleb stood. "Which one is he?"

Elora cleared her throat and turned, meeting Nathan's gaze. "Nathan Campbell, this is my younger sister, Temperance. Nathan is my choice." Then she looked past him. "That man with Declan is his friend, Caleb."

"I'm pleased to meet ye both," Temperance said, her eyes bright with sudden joy. A full smile broke across her lovely face.

The sight cut straight to his heart.

She turned back to face Elora. "I have done as ye requested. The guest chambers have been readied." For a moment, her smiled faltered. "I…I have done well. I do not think ye'll be disappointed."

"I'm sure everything is fine," Elora replied absently.

Caleb came forward then. "Thank ye," he said to Temperance. "But I prefer to sleep in the stables."

Temperance looked to Elora for guidance.

"Of course, Caleb," Elora answered. Then she turned to her younger sister. "Please show Caleb the way."

Nathan watched Elora proceed with confidence and precision as she turned to face the high dais. Following the direction of her gaze, Nathan noticed several serving women waiting dutifully in a line near the high table to carry out their lady's bidding.

"Mary," Elora called. A young maid, as slim as a reed with bright green eyes and brown hair tied back at the nape of her neck came forward and dipped into a low curtsy.

"Aye, my lady."

"Please take Nathan to his chamber." Then Elora turned back to face him. "Ye'll find a change of clothing on the bed. Please dress as quickly as ye can. Mary will await ye outside yer chamber door."

Nathan's gaze darted between the maid and the lady.

He looked down at his boots and plaid, which were, indeed, muddy from their journey but no worse for wear. More confused than ever, he turned, looking for Caleb, but his friend was gone.

"Do not delay," Elora urged him sternly.

He nodded quickly and found himself hurrying after Mary. Clearly, Lady Brodie was in charge of Castle Bròn and everyone in it, and in that moment, he saw no other choice than to follow her command.

~ * ~

Dressed in a clean Brodie plaid and tunic, Nathan stood at the altar of the Brodie kirk with Caleb at his side. The chapel was teeming with villagers who smiled at him and whispered amongst themselves.

Caleb leaned close. "I thought she said she was never going to marry."

Nathan lifted his shoulders. "I thought so, too, but she has appeared to have changed her mind."

Caleb nodded and straightened. Then a moment later, he leaned close again. "And yer certain ye wish to go through with this?"

Nathan looked at the gathering of excited villagers and was struck by a rush of memory. Once upon a time, he had known the love of family and the comfort of belonging to a clan. In that moment, a rare lightness entered his heart. He turned and met Caleb's gaze. "I told ye already. I made up my mind to marry her before we left Edinburgh. I just didn't realize it would happen so soon."

The priest left the sacristy to stand at the altar, and an instant later the doors to the chapel opened and Temperance entered. She was dressed in a violet tunic and silver surcote. Her black curls framed her pale skin and delicate features, and her smile shone brightly. When she walked down the aisle, the villagers smiled in admiration. She stopped across from Caleb and dipped her head in greeting.

Awash in memory, Nathan faltered for a moment at the sight of her, but then the doors opened again, and Elora entered the chapel on Declan's arm, chasing away the ghosts of his past. The lady of Castle Bròn wore a cream-colored tunic under a pale-blue surcote embroidered with pink flowers. Her golden hair had been brushed out and left unbound, and upon her head was a crown of evergreens.

She kept her head downcast as she walked up the aisle. Declan stopped when he reached Nathan. Then he turned to Elora and kissed her cheek before he moved to stand with Murray in the front row.

Nathan waited for Elora to look up, but she kept her gaze downcast. Slowly, she placed her hand on his arm, and together, they moved to stand in front of the priest.

When it was time for Elora to face him, she turned and raised her head, and they locked eyes. He searched her face, but her gaze held no warmth, no feeling. She was more ice queen than bride. But then he noticed her pulse quaking at her neck, and when he reached for her hands as the priest had bidden him, her fingers trembled.

"Ye're beautiful," he whispered.

Pink stole into her cheeks.

He knew then beyond a shadow of a doubt that a vulnerable and complicated woman lived beneath her cold shield.

He leaned close to whisper, "Ye said ye would never marry."

Her brow furrowed. "I meant what I said."

Confused, he gestured to the assembly. "But yer people are here, and a priest. We are going to speak vows—"

"Vows of intent, nothing more."

He raked his hand through his hair. "A simple betrothal need not take place in a church."

"This is no simple betrothal. I want a religious ceremony to strengthen our bond in the eyes of the Mackintosh."

The priest proceeded with Mass, after which they pledged their intent to marry. When they finished, Elora took his hand in hers and turned to face her people. The villagers cheered.

"Ye do know that in the eyes of God and yer people, we are

as good as married," he said for her ears alone.

She turned to face him. "Make no mistake—we have been promised, but that is all. Our union could only be made official if consummated." She paused, giving him a hard look. "Which will never happen." Then she turned quickly on her heel and started to walk back down the aisle.

He admired the sway of her hips for a moment, before slowly, following after. When he stepped out into the courtyard, he watched her greet her people with the dignity of a queen. Women brought their bairns close for her to hold and kiss. She smiled kindly and waved, but her formal manner never faltered.

Joining her, he took hold of her hand. "Ye're still trembling."

She gave him a stern look. "Please keep ye're observations to yerself and remember why I hired ye," she said in a low voice. Then she motioned to Declan and Murray who came forward and began encouraging the people to return to their homes.

"Come along," she said to Nathan. "We still have to sign the contract." Then she started across the courtyard toward the castle doors.

Caleb appeared at his side. "I'm confused. Are ye married then?"

"Nay," Nathan said, watching her hasten up the stairs. "At least, not yet." Once again, he savored the sight of her hips swaying with feminine grace. "We just have one more thing to do."

When he made love to her, he wondered, would she lie beneath him cold and lifeless like polished stone or would the secret fire within her ignite.

A slow smile curved his lips. He couldn't wait to find out.

# Chapter Eight

Elora stood on the battlements of Castle Bròn, gazing out beyond the Brodie village to the line of warriors riding toward them, bearing the colors of Clan Mackintosh.

Flanked by Nathan and Murray, she held fast to her outer composure, even though her heart pounded.

Nathan shielded his eyes from the glare of the sun. "Who is this man? What does he want from ye?"

She fought down her frustration. "I told ye already. Before my father died, he and Egan Mackintosh had begun negotiations for my hand. Egan believes his claim should be honored."

He continued to watch her neighbor's approach. At length, he said, "Is he in love with ye?"

She shook her head. "Like my father, I am certain Laird Mackintosh is incapable of love. He wants to take control of my people, our lands. He wants Clan Brodie for himself."

Then he turned to her. "Tell me more. 'Tis important to know our enemy so that we can take advantage of his weaknesses and prepare for his strengths."

The logic of his words bolstered her courage. She took a deep breath and searched her thoughts. "He desires greater wealth and land above all else, but at the heart of his greed is fear."

"Fear of what?"

"Poverty," Murray chimed in. "When Egan Mackintosh was a child, his clan faced ruination from illness and crop failure. Then tinkers plundered their stores. But his people found no reprieve from suffering. Egan's father was never a strong man, and the struggle broke what little spine he had. The clan continued to suffer even after their land had healed." A distant look came over Murray's face. "I remember when Egan was made laird. His people rejoiced. He brought heart and ambition back to his clan. But as their coffers filled..." Murray shook his head sadly. "It was never enough. He became hard and ruthless, just like..." His voice trailed off as he met Elora's gaze.

"Just like my father," Elora finished for him.

"Aye," Murray said softly.

"He will look for weakness?" Nathan said, knowingly.

"What do ye mean?"

"Greed makes cowards of men. He will run from strength and attack anything he deems as lesser." He turned and met her gaze. "Right now, that means ye."

Her nostrils flared. A rare moment of anger shaped her features. "I am in no way lesser," she snapped.

Nathan looked her dead on. "Ye're a force to be reckoned with Elora Brodie. God's blood, sometimes ye scare even me. Today, I nigh raced up to my chamber to do yer bidding."

His words brought a touch of warmth to cheeks, but then she straightened her back and turned her attention to the coming threat. With her usual composure intact, she asked, "What are ye trying to say?"

He took her hand in his. "I'm saying, ye hold fast to yer control. Do not waver, and we will win this day."

She met the strength in his gaze with a grateful heart. He was everything she needed him to be in that moment, and so much more. He was brave, strong, and intelligent. With Nathan at her side, her plan could actually work.

He offered her his arm. "Mayhap we should await him at the high table."

She nodded her approval. "He will not expect to find someone in my father's chair."

She rested her hand on his arm, and together, they left the battlements behind and made their way downstairs to the solar and then out onto the high dais. Servants rushed to and fro, preparing for their betrothal feast.

"My lady," Nathan said, drawing her gaze. He had pulled out her chair.

"Thank ye," she said, claiming her rightful seat.

"May I," he asked, gesturing to what had once been her father's place.

She nodded. "For the duration of yer stay, consider this chair yers."

He put his hand on the arm of the intricately carved, high back chair. For a moment, a breath, she saw a shadow of pain cross his features, but it was gone in a flash. Once again, his keen silver eyes and cool composure surfaced.

He sat beside her and took her hand. "Do not let him see yer fear."

"Life under my father's rule taught me how to conceal my true feelings."

"Ye're composure is unmatched, but..." His words trailed off.

She met his gaze. "But what?"

"Yer face and eyes are unreadable, but ye clench yer fists when ye're angry or afraid."

She looked down at her lap and her breath caught. Her

hands gripped her tunic in tight fists. "Ye're right." She took a deep breath and slowly softened her fingers. "I had no idea." Her heart started to pound. She touched her flushed cheeks. Fighting for calm, she could feel herself beginning to unravel.

"Look at me," Nathan said firmly. "I did not tell ye that to unnerve ye. I told ye that because I want ye to succeed. I may not know much about ye or yer clan, but in the few hours that I have been on Brodie land, one thing is clear. Clan Brodie is devoted to their lady. I also know that true devotion only comes to the deserving." He cupped her cheeks between his hands. "Ye can do this. Ye said so yerself just now on the battlements. Ye're in no way lesser."

"He's right, my lady," Declan said, coming up the stairs to take his place at the high table.

She nodded, took a deep breath, closed her eyes, and focused on easing the tension from her body. Then, after stretching her neck from side to side, she met Nathan's gaze. "I'm ready."

A noise behind her drew her gaze as Temperance walked onto the high dais with Caleb at her side.

Declan stood and motioned to her sister. "Tempest, take the seat next to yer sister. I will move down one."

Nathan leaned close and whispered. "Why did Declan call yer sister Tempest?"

Elora looked at her sister's flushed cheeks and darting eyes. "I've no doubt ye will learn why soon enough."

"I'm so nervous," Temperance said when she sat down.

Elora met her sister's deep-blue gaze. "All will be fine. Just keep breathing, and for pity's sake, hold tight to yer temper." Then she noticed Caleb beginning to descend the stairs down to the main floor. "Nay, Caleb," she called. "Please take yer place beside Nathan. As far as anyone knows, ye're his kinsman."

Nodding, Caleb hastened back and took his seat. A moment later, the doors swung open, and Murray entered the great hall, followed by a dozen Brodie warriors. Behind them, Laird Mackintosh and his warriors entered.

Egan Mackintosh was a formidable man of great height with a thick sinewy neck. Silver threaded his black hair, which was cropped short, and he wore his beard in a plait that hung down to his wide chest. Over his plaid, a fur-lined black cloak draped his broad shoulders and billowed out behind him as he marched through the doorway.

Smiling confidently, he locked eyes with Elora, but froze mid-step an instant later.

A thrill shot up Elora's spine, for she knew Egan had noticed Nathan occupying the laird's place at the high table.

Egan's smile vanished. His eyes narrowed. He stormed toward the high dais with clenched fists.

"Who is this man?" he thundered.

Elora stood with unrushed grace. "Welcome, Laird Mackintosh. May I offer ye and yer men some refreshment after yer journey here."

His nostrils flared. "I have asked ye a question."

Elora pressed her hand to her chest. "How remiss of me. Of course, introductions must come first. Laird Mackintosh, 'tis my pleasure to present to ye Nathan Campbell...my betrothed."

Egan's face reddened and his eyes flashed wide "That is a lie!"

Nathan stood slowly. "There's no need to yell," he said, his own voice deadly soft.

"Who are ye?" Egan growled.

"My lady has already given ye an answer."

"I demand to see a contract!"

Declan slid the parchment in front of Nathan. He picked it

up and stood, leaning over the high table to hand it to Egan. "See for yerself."

Egan closed the distance in a few angry steps and snatched the paper from Nathan's hand. "This is impossible."

Elora stood. "We spoke our vows in the kirk before God, Father Paul, and my people."

Egan scanned the page, his face deepening in color as he read. But then he slowly looked up as the scowl retreated from his brow. He held up his hand, revealing an ink smudge on his thumb. "The ink is still wet," he smirked. "This was signed only today."

"Whether today, yesterday, or a fortnight ago, it makes no difference," Elora said coolly. "The contract is binding."

He crumpled the parchment in his fist. "My claim comes first. Yer father—"

Temperance jumped to her feet. "My father is dead! Ye have no contract!"

"Thank ye," Elora said to her sister. "Now, please sit down." Then she turned back to Egan. "Temperance is right. There was never a contract to prove yer claim."

"Ye have done this to vex me," Egan shouted. "But I see through this ploy of yers!"

"I have chosen a husband," Elora answered calmly. "That 'tis all."

"I don't believe ye," Egan growled. "Why did ye not marry him? What reason have ye to delay?"

Her heart lodged in her throat. It was all she could do not to clench her fists. She wanted to delay the wedding because she did not wish to marry any man, but she could not tell Egan this.

Nathan pressed his hands on the table. "Do not doubt our intent. We wait only for the Lenten season to pass."

Inside, her heart leapt, but she was careful to conceal her emotions. "'Tis only proper," she chimed in. "Now then, if ye and yer men would like to stay, ye may join us for our betrothal feast."

Egan gave her an assessing look as he handed the contract back to her. "For weeks ye have been dismissing my claim, but ye never once mentioned…" his voice trailed off. "What is yer name?"

"Nathan Campbell."

"And who is yer father?"

"He is chieftain of Clan Campbell to the north."

A slow smile spread across his face. "Are ye his heir?"

Nathan shook his head. "I am third in line."

Egan's eyes flashed with anger. "Ye bring to this alliance no land, no fortune!"

"I am in possession of a fortune, but one which I have earned with my own sweat. But ours is not a match of convenience or duty." He wrapped his arm around her waist and gently pulled her to his side. "We are in love."

"She's as frigid as a winter morn," Egan sneered. "Clan Brodie's ice queen is not capable of love."

A choir of swords unsheathing rent the air as the Brodie warriors reacted to hearing their lady insulted. An instant later, the Mackintosh warriors armed themselves.

"Hold!" Elora called, her voice strong and steady. She raised her brow at Egan. Then she turned on her heel and walked the length of the high dais. Head high, shoulders back, she descended to the main floor and closed the distance between her and the laird. Silence hung thick in the air as she held his gaze for several moments, her composure never faltering. "Ye're hardly an expert on such matters." Then she motioned to Mary who held a serving tray gripped tight in her hand, staring with mouth agape. It took her a moment to respond, but then she nodded and hastened to Elora's side.

Elora grasped a tankard from the tray and offered it to her neighbor. "It would be a shame to come all this way and not partake in our feast."

He glared at her. "Ye may have fooled that love-sick sod and yer adoring kinfolk, but do not think for a moment that I do not know the truth. Ye have done this to nullify my claim."

She felt her fingers wish to close tight, but again she resisted. "Yer claim was never made binding."

He drew close, a sneer twisting his weathered face. "I know what is in yer heart. Ye've never been agreeable to marriage, and now ye expect me to believe that ye're suddenly in love. A woman cannot protect this clan."

She held his gaze with unfailing confidence. "Take yer cup and sit down with yer men, for tonight is my betrothal celebration. Ye've darkened this joyous day enough. Unless ye wish to find out how well my warriors respond to taking orders from a woman, I suggest ye do as I have bidden."

Egan's nostrils flared, but he reached out and accepted the cup. Slowly, the anger melted from his face, replaced by a shrewd smile. "I wouldn't dream of missing such an occasion. The only day I'm looking forward to more is yer wedding day."

Then he jerked his head to his men, and together they filled one of the trestle tables.

His final words sunk in her mind, causing trepidation to take root, but with graceful ease, head held high, she climbed the steps to the high table. Nathan stretched out his hand to her. When she slipped her hand in his, she could see his approval of her performance in his eyes.

With a deep breath, she took her seat. "Declan, give orders to open the gate. Let the villagers come."

She sat straight in her seat and watched the evening unfold. Her kinfolk gathered around the trestle tables and helped themselves to trenchers teeming with fried fish and stacks of bannock. Everything was running smoothly. Even Egan and his men kept silent. All was going as planned. At least for that moment, her hold on Clan Brodie and her own independence was strong.

"My lady," someone cried.

Elora stood and scanned the tables and spied one of the oldest members of her clan, Hamish. His gnarled hand gripped a tankard high, and he beamed at her. "A kiss!"

Elora laughed. "Ye funny old sod," she called. "Ye must come here if ye want a kiss."

He laughed. "I'll take my kiss the next time ye make the rounds. I meant for yer betrothed."

Beneath the table, away from everyone's gaze, her hands clenched in tight fists.

A kiss.

She had never kissed a man before.

She could feel her composure slipping away. And then suddenly, Nathan took her hand and pulled her to her feet. They locked eyes. His silver gaze bore into hers, and in that moment the din of the great hall grew distant to her ears. He pulled her close and tenderly cupped her cheek. Then he slowly lowered his lips to hers. His touch was feather soft. Her chest tightened as sensation shot up her stiff spine. She tentatively placed her hands on his shoulders and felt her rigid body soften as if of its own accord. He held her closer still, and a sweet ache coursed through her, igniting that place within, which she never let too close to the surface. His taste, his smell, the feel of his muscular shoulders flexing beneath her fingertips—it was all too much.

Just when she thought she couldn't take any more, he released her. She stumbled back slightly.

The room erupted into cheers.

He wrapped his arm around her waist and turned so that they faced her people.

"Smile," he said under his breath, bringing her back to her senses.

She smiled and waved. Then Clan Brodie came forward with betrothal gifts of honey, wood carvings, embroidered handkerchiefs, and dried flowers. She thanked each of her kin with the same grace and dignity that she brought to everything she did, but on the inside, her soul was on fire.

She could still feel Nathan's mouth on hers, his tongue grazing her lips, his strong arms surrounding her, filling her with desire.

Frustration fought to rise to the surface, threatening her calm.

Just when she thought she finally had everything under control, Nathan had kissed her, proving how susceptible she was to his touch. How could one man threaten her composure so much? Determined to guard her emotions more closely, she took a deep breath and pushed her shoulders back.

Doubtless, she had hired the right man. They worked well together, and he had proven himself more useful than she would have dared dream possible when she first laid eyes on him in The Devil's Bridge.

In the short time she had known Nathan, she had witnessed his goodness and intelligence, but also his reckless and indulgent nature. More than that, he was a man who was used to being in command. Strengthening her resolve, she reminded herself that the best thing for her and her people was for her to remain the leader of Clan Brodie.

After all, she did not need a man...even one who could stir her soul with his kiss.

# Chapter Nine

Nathan scanned the great hall. Long had it been since he had sat at the high table and watched the revelry of kinfolk. He glanced over at his betrothed. As always, she was unreadable, with her stoic expression and straight spine. Her attention never wavered from her duties. With a simple nod of her head or a gesture of her delicate, white hand, the evening progressed smoothly, the castle servants always in accord with their lady's wishes.

When everyone had eaten their fill, she bade the pipers play while men from the clan came together and pushed several of the trestle tables off to the side. After clearing a large space in front of the high dais, the merrymaking began.

Elora sat at his side, reservedly clapping her hands while her kinfolk kicked up their heels and circled in reels to the music. Meanwhile, Temperance swayed in her seat to the tune, her black curls bouncing and her face beaming brightly. At the start of the second song, Elora's younger sister lunged to her feet. "May I join the dancing, Elora?"

"Aye, my dear, only try to remember that ye're a lady of Clan Brodie."

"I will!" Temperance threw her arms around Elora's neck and

pressed a fleeting kiss to her cheek. Hitching up her tunic, she nigh sprinted the length of the high dais and down the stairs to join the other dancers.

Nathan leaned close and in a low voice said to Elora, "I'm beginning to see why some call her Tempest."

Elora nodded smoothly in reply but did not look his way. In fact, she hadn't spoken to him or met his gaze since he had pulled her close in answer to her elderly kinsman's request. His thoughts drifted back to that moment as he remembered her innocent response to his kiss. At first, she had been stiff, but then she melted ever so slightly into his embrace, giving him a taste of the passion he knew lay hidden beneath her armor of decorum.

But now her bearing was stonier than ever.

He cast his gaze toward the table of Mackintosh warriors to ensure Egan was not aggravating her. But he and two of his men were hunched over, speaking in low voices, paying no heed to the high table or the surrounding revelry.

Nathan cleared his throat, and once again leaned close to Elora. "Would ye like to join in the dance?"

This time, she turned and faced him. Her gaze held no warmth. "I do not dance," she said simply, then looked away.

Nathan straightened in his seat, marveling at her continued restraint. Still, a slight smile curved his lips. Try as she might to maintain her indifference toward him, he knew better. He had felt her response. For a fleeting moment, her emotions had escaped the fortress of her self-control.

Mary suddenly appeared in front of the high table and dipped in a quick curtsy. "My lady, Hamish has requested yer company." Then with a wink, she said, "I think he wishes to collect the kiss ye promised him."

A controlled smile upturned Elora's lips. "Tell him that he may join me here and take my sister's seat."

Mary's smile faltered. "Did ye not hear?"

Elora stiffened. "What is it?"

"Hamish twisted his ankle while ye were away. He cannot walk. Declan had to carry him here."

Concern wrinkling her brow, Elora did not hesitate. She stood and without a parting word to Nathan, hurried away to check on her elderly kinsman.

Nathan's gaze followed her across the room. As always, she glided, even in her haste. When she reached the old man, his face lit up to see his lady. Elora smiled, only this time her eyes were imbued with warmth. Again, he glimpsed the soul she so carefully guarded.

Would she ever look at him that way?

Stiffening in his seat, he shook the thought from his head and reminded himself why he had agreed to her plan in the first place. He was after the Brodie chiefdom, not her heart.

Forcing his gaze away from her elegant beauty, he turned his attention to the dancers. Temperance skipped close to their table. Her laughter rang out while she kicked up her heels. Her cheeks were flushed. She emanated joy. The sight made his chest tighten. Reaching for his ale, he downed the lot.

"Ye ken what I can't understand?" Caleb said suddenly in a low voice at his side.

Nathan set his empty tankard down and waited for Caleb to continue.

"What we're doing here."

Nathan met Caleb's keen blue eyes. "I'm marrying Elora so that I can be laird."

Caleb gave him an appraising look. "For years, I have ridden

71

with ye. Never once have ye sought advancement of this kind. In fact, do ye remember when we tracked down that blackguard who stole Baron Clifford's prize horse? Do ye remember his offer?"

Nathan scratched at his chin. "Aye, that was last spring, and if I remember correctly, he paid us one-hundred silver pieces for the job."

"Two-hundred, actually, but only after he offered ye land and a title."

Nathan shrugged. "What good does an English title and land do me?"

Caleb threw his hands up. "Plenty!"

"I am a Highlander, not some border lord. But now I have a chance to be laird. Most men wouldn't question my interest. What if ye had the same offer? Would ye turn down a chiefdom?"

"Aye," Caleb said simply. "I would."

Nathan lifted his shoulders. "'Tis fortuitous then that 'tis I who have been given this opportunity."

Caleb rubbed the back of his neck. "I just…I just think ye're chasing ghosts."

Nathan waved away his friend's concern. "This is no different than any other job, except the prize, which is beyond compare. And ye shall profit also, my friend."

Caleb expelled a slow breath, then lifted his shoulders in surrender. "If this is what ye want, then ye and I both know that eventually she will have to wed. Just be sure 'tis ye she chooses in the end."

Just then, Temperance rushed up to the table, her brow drawn with concern. "Where is Elora?"

Tension flooded Nathan's shoulders as he looked into Temperance's worried face. "She is speaking with Hamish," he said gently.

A look of relief washed over her. "When I noticed her empty chair, I grew nervous." She glanced over at Elora and, once more, a smile lit up her face. Her worry forgotten, she turned back to Nathan. "Come and dance!"

"Not right now, but thank ye," he replied.

"I hope ye're not waiting for Elora to join in. She never dances."

Nathan sat back in his chair. "Another thing she and I have in common." Then he gestured to Caleb. "But my friend here lives for a good dance."

Temperance's eyes lit up. "Come on then, Caleb!"

Caleb sat unmoving.

"Please!" Temperance said, batting her lovely blue eyes.

Slowly Caleb stood. "Ye owe me," he said in a low voice to Nathan before he walked the length of the high dais and met Temperance at the foot of the stairs. She seized his hand and pulled him into a reel.

Nathan claimed his friend's full tankard and raised it high. "'Tis good for ye, ye unsociable bugger!" His laughter trailed off. He was alone at the high table. A hollowness settled in his chest as he watched the surrounding gaiety. Caleb and Temperance danced past, and Temperance waved at him, her smile shining brightly.

A mirthless laugh fled his lips before he took a long draught of ale. Caleb had been wrong. He wasn't chasing ghosts. It was the other way around.

Ghosts were after him.

"I wish to retire."

He had not noticed Elora's return. Shifting in his seat, he

looked up, meeting her clear blue gaze.

"So soon? 'Tis our wedding feast after all."

"Betrothal feast," she corrected him.

He stood up. "Am I to escort ye to yer chamber?"

She nodded, her face impassive.

He finished his ale and offered her his arm. "Good. Now I will know where yer chamber is."

Her stony expression remained unchanged.

"'Twas a jest," he added. "Do we need to announce our departure?"

She placed her hand on his arm. "I have already spoken with Murray and Declan. I wish to slip away and let the celebration continue."

Together, they retreated to the back of the high dais and behind the screen, which hid the passage to the family rooms.

When they were alone in the hallway, he asked the question weighing most on his mind. "What will ye do when Lent is over? Laird Mackintosh will return when he doesn't receive a wedding invitation."

She raised her chin higher. "Ye needn't concern yerself."

He guessed by her answer that she had no ready solution. "'Tis a fortnight from now. I'm sure ye'll think of something by then."

"Given yer taste for indulgence, I'm surprised ye know the dates of the Lenten season." She looked pointedly at the tankard of ale still gripped in his other hand. "I assume ye've not given anything up."

He raised a brow at her haughty tone. "I was going to refrain from the company of uptight noblewomen, but I decided to make an exception for ye."

She stiffened at his side. Then she turned to face him. Her

nostrils flared, but it was not anger he glimpsed in her eyes. He'd hurt her.

Before she could voice her displeasure, he drew close and cupped her cheek. "I didn't mean that. Forgive me."

She swallowed hard, and an instant later, he could see her composure return. "I was also in the wrong. I should not have criticized ye." She started forward again. They ascended the large stairwell. "'Tis imperative that we, at least, in appearance think well of each other." She gave him a pointed look when they reached the landing. "Especially now that ye've declared to all the world that we're in love."

A smile spread slowly across his face. "I was trying to help. Forgive me for saying so, but ye seemed unprepared to answer some of his questions."

She lifted her shoulders. "I was. I hatched this scheme, quite honestly, out of desperation not even a month ago. Only Declan, Murray, and Temperance know the truth. It probably won't surprise ye to know that neither of the men approved at first." Her face lightened as she continued, "but they both took me aside just now and told me that my plan was going well. I've no doubt yer quick thinking earlier with Egan has fueled their sudden confidence."

He smiled at her praise. "We make a fine team, I think."

She neither agreed nor disagreed with him, but she held his gaze. And, for a moment, her countenance was easy as if she might be conversing with an old friend and not a scoundrel she'd hired for a job.

"Come along," she said, her voice kind. "We are almost to my chamber."

They walked in comfortable silence. When she stopped in front of a door, he took in his surroundings to ensure he remembered which chamber was hers. Then he bowed to her.

"Goodnight, my lady," he said softly before opening the door for her.

She entered and turned to face him and held his gaze. Her expression was still guarded, but her features were soft. "Goodnight, Nathan."

She slowly closed the door.

He reached out and flattened his palm on the wood. "Until the morrow," he whispered.

Then he backed away and looked at the half-finished tankard of ale in his hand. Shaking his head, he walked down the hallway. There was a table on the landing. He stood there for a moment, gripping the tankard. Then, with a deep breath, he set his drink down and walked away.

If he was going to win Elora's hand, he needed to be a better man.

# Chapter Ten

E lora opened her eyes. Stretching her arms over her head, she savored the comfort of her own bed. Hazy and unguarded, her thoughts turned to the kiss she and Nathan had shared, to his silver eyes, and strong hands. Her memory traced the shape of his sideways smile, which had lingered on his lips as she slowly closed her chamber door.

"Stop it," she said aloud before turning her face into her pillow to smother the blush that sought to warm her cheeks. Then she lay on her back again and looked up at the ceiling.

Certainly, he was appealing, but what did that matter? Nathan wasn't the first handsome man she had ever laid eyes on. Caleb, with his long black hair, strong jaw, and deep-set blue eyes, was equally as fine to look upon as were several of her kinsmen.

An ache settled in her chest.

Nathan was different.

There was something in his gaze, something she couldn't name, that held hers captive, something she had glimpsed right from the start.

"Enough," she muttered, trying to force him from her thoughts. Instead, she reflected on how well the confrontation with Egan had gone, but that only led her thoughts straight back to Nathan. There was no denying that yesterday's success was, in no small part, owed to his quick thinking. He was shrewd and observant, not to mention brave and—

A knock sounded at the door.

"Come in," she blurted, grateful for a distraction.

Mary walked into the room, carrying Elora's customary morning tray, which she set on the table near the hearth.

"What is the hour, Mary?"

"'Tis *Lauds*," she smiled.

Elora stood, crossed to her casement, and opened the shutters. She nodded her approval at the sun breaking over the horizon, casting beams of color across the sky. She breathed deep the crisp morning air.

"Come sit, and break yer fast, my lady," Mary bade her. "Then ye can make yer list."

Just hearing Mary speak the word 'list' brought peace to Elora's soul. A day spent immersed in duty would cleanse away her frivolous thoughts. Feeling inwardly content, she sat down and, just as she did every morning, she spread a thin layer of butter on a warm bannock. Having started the last several days with a strip of dried meat, she closed her eyes to savor the first bite, but that was all the idleness she allowed herself. She quickly finished her breakfast, washing the bannock down with a small cup of milk.

"Here ye are, my lady," Mary said, handing her a damp cloth to clean her fingers.

"Thank ye."

Mary removed the tray, setting it on the floor by the door. Then she turned back around and withdrew a small piece of parchment that she had tucked in the waist of her apron and spread it out on the table. "I will fetch yer ink and quill."

"Thank ye."

"I imagine today's list is going to be a long one."

Elora nodded. "Not only have I been gone for days, but we have much to do to set the castle right after yesterday's feast, not to mention our guests."

A slight smile curved Mary's lip. "Don't ye mean yer betrothed?"

Elora looked away to hide the pink she knew suddenly colored her cheeks. After a few moments, she turned back to face her maid, confident that the moment of weakness had passed. "Of course, I meant Nathan and his kinsman, Caleb, but no doubt Egan and his men will want to break their fast—"

"Forgive me for interrupting, my lady," Mary chimed in. "But Laird Mackintosh and his men left before daybreak."

She paused and looked up from her list making. "Egan is gone? Are ye certain?"

"Aye, my lady. I was helping wee Thomas rekindle the hearth in the great hall, he still struggles with the wood bin, sweet dear, when Laird Mackintosh came downstairs and roused his men. In no time at all, they marched out to the courtyard."

Skeptical that she could be rid of Egan so soon, Elora chewed her lip. "They may have just gone into the village."

Mary shook her head. "Nay, my lady. After they left the great hall, I bade Thomas finish up on his own, and I hastened to the battlements to see where they went. And sure enough, they gathered their horses from the stables and rode on their way. I saw them crest the hill beyond the fields."

"Ye're certain?"

"I saw them with my own eyes."

Egan was already gone!

She allowed herself a long exhale. "Well done, Mary!"

Elora's praise made her young maid blush.

With fresh resolve, Elora gripped her quill and dipped the tip in ink. "This is proving to be a fine day, indeed. Now, let us get back to work."

Mary nodded eagerly.

"I must take full account of the pantry to see what needs to be replenished after yesterday's feast." Elora scribbled that down. "And before I left for Edinburgh, the stable master wanted to discuss repairing the holding coral." She made her note. "And I mustn't forget Hamish. I must ensure he is cared for and has everything he needs." Then she added several daily chores to her list before she set her quill down. "That is all for now."

"Very well, my lady."

Elora stood ready to face the day. "Shall we begin?"

Mary turned on her heel and crossed the room to Elora's wardrobe. She opened the door and pulled out a deep blue tunic and silver surcote embroidered with a delicate row of white flowers around the collar.

After Mary helped her dress, she brushed out Elora's hair and separated her thick flaxen curls into three sections, which she plaited. Then she coiled the plaits on top of Elora's head, using countless pins to hold her heavy tresses in place.

"Ye look lovely, my lady."

Elora pulled at the cuffs to ensure the sleeves did not wrinkle before nodding with approval at her neat appearance in the mirror. Turning away, she paused to listen when the chapel bell sounded the hour of *Prime*. "We're right on schedule." Taking a deep breath, she crossed the room, savoring her well-ordered world. "Let us go to work."

Murray was awaiting her in the solar just as he did every morning. He showed her the recent adjustments to the accounts and told her about a dispute he had to settle while she was away. When they finished, she thanked him for his prudence and faithful service. Then she made her way to the kitchen.

The cook, Agnes, was a tall woman with a sturdy build, ruddy complexion, and bright red hair, which she wore twisted in a high knot on her head. At that moment, Agnes was meeting with her team of undercooks, discussing the day's menu; meanwhile, several of the younger serving children were helping with the wash and other chores. She spied wee Thomas carrying a bucket of water. He was a lad of six with auburn hair and a smattering of freckles across his cheeks.

"Well done, Thomas! My, how strong ye've grown."

A smile rounded the apples of his freckled cheeks before his bashful gaze dropped to the floor.

"Good morrow, my lady," Agnes said, meeting her gaze. The older woman dipped into a low curtsy and was soon joined by the other cooks.

"Good morrow," Elora said in greeting on her way to the pantry. "Do not stop on my account."

She opened the pantry door and smiled in greeting at Castle Bròn's pantler.

"I thought I would see ye today," Alison said looking up from the basket she was holding, which contained several round loaves of bread.

Elora smiled at the young woman.

Alison was three and twenty. She had glossy blond curls, warm green eyes, and her cheeks dimpled when she smiled. Her mother, who had been the castle's pantler for more than five and twenty years, had passed away two years ago from a fever that had ravaged the clan, claiming more than a dozen lives.

"How are ye feeling?" Elora asked, looking pointedly at Alison's swollen stomach.

"Fat," Alison said cheerfully. "She's a strong lass to be sure. Kept me up half the night with all her kicks and shifting about, but the kitchen lads are as helpful as ever. They're saving me from having to lift too much."

Elora nodded with approval, then she opened the log and began to scan the shelves, marking what was used and what was needed; meanwhile, Alison called out additional numbers as she loaded fresh bread, eggs, and cheese onto the shelves.

When the hour neared *Terce*, a knock sounded at the pantry door, and Temperance peered inside. "Elora, will ye come for a ride with me?"

"I'm too busy," Elora answered absently as she reviewed the number of loaves sent to the table the day before. "Take Firtha instead."

"She will tire too quickly and complain all the while about her aching rear."

Firtha, Temperance's dressing maid, was tall and slim as a reed. She had black hair, a long, narrow face, and brown eyes framed by thick dark brows that were almost always pinched with worry. She fretted constantly, which was why Elora had thought to pair her with Temperance.

"Ask Declan."

"He is busy."

"Two bushels of apples," Elora said aloud as she wrote before answering her sister. "Ye'll have to make do. I simply do not have time now."

"Ye never do."

Elora looked up and met Temperance's disappointed gaze. "Ye aren't a child anymore, Temperance. I cannot cease my duties each time a whim strikes ye. Go to the solar and work on yer tapestry. When I am finished here, we shall break for dinner and then take a short ride."

Temperance opened her mouth as if to ask Elora to reconsider, but then she sighed and shut the door.

"She's a spirited lass, yer sister," Alison said softly.

Elora nodded. "Aye, she is. I wish she would learn some restraint."

A moment later, another knock sounded.

Elora straightened. "What does she want now?"

But it was Declan who opened the door. "What has happened?" he began, "Tempest just fled the kitchen with tears in her eyes. She didn't stop when I asked what was wrong."

Elora gave a wave of her hand, shifting her gaze back to the shelves. "She'll be fine. What do ye need, Declan?"

"With yer permission, I will make the rounds and visit the outlying cottars."

She nodded her approval. "Thank ye," she said absently. "I would appreciate that."

"And if ye do not object, I will bring Nathan and Caleb."

She whirled around to face him. "Whatever for?" Straightaway, she locked eyes with Nathan who was now standing in the doorway behind the captain of her guard. Her heart started to race at the sight of him, and it all came hurtling back at her. Clinging to her composure, she steeled her shoulders. "Good morrow," she said, her voice steady.

"Good morrow," he answered, canting his head to the side. His thoughtful gaze held hers. At length, he continued in a soft voice. "I've not seen ye today."

Her stomach fluttered, but she fought for calm. "My duties are many."

"Then ye've been busy." He gave her his lazy sideways smile. "I'm glad to know ye've not been avoiding me."

She was busy, but of course, she had also been avoiding him, although she was certainly not going to admit as much to him. He needn't know how tumultuous her deeply buried feelings were.

Silence hung in the air.

At length, Declan came forward again. "We will leave then if there is nothing else ye require, my lady."

"I do require something." Her casual tone belied her racing heart.

Declan looked at her expectantly.

"A word with ye in private."

Nathan met her gaze. She could see a series of emotions pass his face, none of which she was willing to reflect upon long enough to identify. Then he slowly backed away from the doorway. Without a word, Alison also took her leave.

Then she whirled to face Declan. "Why would ye seek to take Nathan with ye?"

He lifted his shoulders. "I wanted to show him our lands."

Her hands settled on her hips. "He's a thief-taker, remember, no better than a common criminal. Ye said so yerself."

The older man blushed. "I know I said that but after what transpired here with Egan, not to mention how he aided our journey home..." Declan raked a hand through his silver-threaded hair. "He has impressed me with his keen thinking."

"I am not going to marry him!"

Declan's eyes widened. "I was not trying to imply that ye should. I was simply trying to say that I have come to admire him. I enjoy his company, and I thought it might be a hospitable thing to do."

She tilted her chin higher. "Well, then…I suppose it would be all right if he joined ye."

He dipped his head to her. "Thank ye, my lady."

"When will ye return?"

"Expect us late tomorrow evening."

She nodded her approval. "Take what ye need from our stores for the cottars. Just be sure to tell Murray so that he can mark it down."

"I will, my lady. Be careful while we're away."

She smiled reassuringly. "Ye needn't fash yerself, Declan. I'm always careful."

He bowed to her, then turned and left the pantry.

Standing alone, her chest started to tighten, and an inexplicable hollowness settled in the pit of her stomach. Without thinking, she raced from the pantry into the kitchen.

"My lady," Agnes exclaimed with wide eyes. "All ye all right? I've never seen ye rush so."

"I'm fine," she said absently while she quickly scanned the kitchen.

The men had already left.

She started toward the kitchen door to chase after them, but then she froze. In that moment, she realized why she had the sudden urge to track them down.

She wanted to bid Nathan farewell.

Swallowing hard, she closed her eyes and took a deep breath. Then she turned on her heel and retreated back to the pantry.

"My lady," Alison said, looking up from where she sat perched on a stack of grain sacks. "I can finish here, if ye wish to join yer betrothed."

"Thank ye, Alison. That is very considerate of ye, but I've been gone from Bròn for too long as it is. Nathan will be in

85

good hands with Declan."

Alison looked at her curiously at first, but then she smiled and said, "As ye wish, my lady."

Elora turned away from Alison's probing gaze, pretending to be occupied with counting the stacks of cheese wheels, but, in truth, she was trying to keep herself from unraveling. She took a deep breath, forcing her heart to cease its racing.

Nathan was gone and would not return for nigh on two days. She straightened her back and forbade the sadness that kept trying to pull at her heart. Shaking her head, she dismissed her feelings as nothing more than fatigue. Now, at least she would have peace from it all—Egan's claim, her plan of last resort, her temporary betrothed. And in that time, she would set things right at Bròn, make the rounds throughout the village, and rid her mind of the blasted yearning that now filled her thoughts.

# Chapter Eleven

Bound for the outer realms of Brodie Territory, Nathan sat beside Declan who drove the wagon; meanwhile, Caleb rode his black mount alongside. Spring was beginning to awaken the ground. Vibrant green shoots dotted the moorland, peeking out amid the faded bracken and jutting rocks.

"'Tis our first stop," Declan said, pointing to a cottage in the distance. "'Tis the home of a jolly couple who will no doubt be pleased by our company, but ye'd best warn Caleb—they have three unwed daughters."

Nathan smiled. "We'll let that be a surprise, shall we?"

His gaze traced the smoke that coiled out from the cottage's thatched rooftop in thick billowing ribbons. Then he shifted in his seat and glanced back at the bed of the wagon, which was teeming with stacks of cheese wheels, baskets of crusty bread, and burlap sacks filled with milled oats. "I used to make the rounds with my father and brothers when I was a lad," he said absently.

As the wagon bumped along, Declan cleared his throat, drawing Nathan's gaze. "I ken 'tis not my place," the older man began, "but may I ask why ye left yer clan?"

Nathan's chest tightened. He was not prepared to answer questions about his past. After all, for years he had done everything he could to forget—drinking, women. And for the most part, he had succeeded, except for when night came, and his dreams brought it all back. Silence hung in the air. Then at length, he posed his own question to change the subject. "How many cottars are spread across these lands?"

"Three and twenty families live beyond the boundaries of Brodie village," Declan answered.

He waited tensely for Declan to continue his line of questioning, but the older man did not press Nathan, for which he was grateful.

When they reached the edge of a partially plowed field, Nathan spied a broad shouldered man with wild black curls and a fluffy beard. His thick arms flexed with rugged strength as he drove a pair of oxen forward, turning the soil. When he noticed their approach, he pulled on the reins to stop the great beasts and called out, "Good day, Declan!"

Smiling, Declan jerked on the reins, bringing the wagon to a halt. Then the captain jumped down and clasped the cottar's outstretched hand. "Good day, Fergus! How are ye and all yer beautiful lassies?"

Fergus's leathery face broke into a smile. "We're well and blessed to be so."

"Declan!"

Nathan shifted his gaze toward the cottage. A smiling woman with a weathered complexion came running out from the cottage, her chestnut hair flowing like a cape behind her. When she drew close enough, she nigh threw herself at Declan, squeezing him, her face straining from the effort.

Declan chuckled. "I can't quite breath, Aileen."

Fergus threw his head back with laughter. "Let the captain go, wife, before he faints dead away."

Laughing, Aileen did as her husband had bidden her, but then her laughter faltered as she looked beyond Declan, her gaze settling first on Nathan and then Caleb. "Who have ye brought with ye?"

"Allow me to introduce Nathan Campbell and his kinsman, Caleb," Declan began. He hesitated for a moment before continuing, "Nathan and Lady Elora are betrothed."

Aileen's eyes flashed wide. "Praise be to all the Saints! Come on then," she said, motioning for Nathan to come closer. "Let's have a look at ye."

Nathan climbed down from the wagon to greet the cottars properly, but before he knew what was happening, Aileen closed the distance between them and seized him in a crushing embrace. At length, she drew back a little and looked up at his face. "Broad shoulders, silver eyes, white teeth, I can see why ye won our lady over." Then she glanced over at his friend. "And yer kinsman is also gentle on the eyes." She called over to Caleb. "Are ye married?"

"Not that I'm aware of," Caleb answered, which bent Aileen over with laughter.

"My daughters have just gone to fetch some water. Two are of age," she added with a wink.

Declan came forward, a smile crinkling the skin around his eyes. "Unfortunately, we cannot linger, Aileen. Ye'll have to give our respect to yer daughters."

She looked pointedly at Caleb, "Don't think I won't." Then, once more, she crushed Declan close. "Ye tell our lady I expect to see her soon."

Declan smiled down at the Aileen's cheerful face. "I'm certain that she'll make the rounds soon."

"Ye be sure to come along." Aileen said to Nathan. "And bring yer kinsman," she added, flashing a bright smile at Caleb.

"I wouldn't be able to keep him away," Nathan began, shooting a quick glance at his friend. "He's a sociable sort of fellow, to be sure. Aren't ye, Caleb?"

Caleb cocked a brow at Nathan, but he smiled amiably at Aileen and answered, "Indeed."

Chuckling, Declan seized a bag of grain, loaves of bread, and a wheel of cheese and filled the cottars' arms. Then he said, "We'd best be off, men."

Fergus and Aileen called out words of gratitude, bidding them farewell as they rolled away, the wagon bumping over the rocky earth.

The rest of the day passed in much the same way, journeying from cottage to cottage, handing out supplies, checking on the cottars' welfare, and spreading word of their lady's betrothal. Nathan was welcomed wholeheartedly by her kin whose devotion to each other and their lady was unmatched by anything Nathan had ever experienced.

~ * ~

When night fell, they built a fire and laid out pallets beneath the stars. Nathan lay awake for some time, gazing up at the heavens and thinking about the last night he had slept out of doors with Elora tucked securely in his arms. At first, she had lain stiffly, resisting his aid, but then she surrendered to his warmth. Her body had softened, melting into his embrace. Closing his eyes, he could still smell her hair and feel her feminine curves. But the softness had not lasted. By the next morning, she had resurrected the shields around her thoughts and heart.

Now, lying on Brodie soil, beneath a blanket of stars, he wondered whether he would ever come to know the woman hidden behind the polished stone wall that she had so skillfully erected. With unanswered questions racking his brain and the memory of her softness filling his arms, he, at last, drifted off to sleep.

~ * ~

The next morning, they awoke before dawn and set out. After several stops, they reached the coast by midday. The Moray firth stretched out before them. They unhitched the horses to let them graze at the craggy bracken. Then, while Caleb chose a solitary walk, Nathan and Declan headed down to the shore. Picking up a smooth stone, Nathan threw it beyond the rocks jutting up from the waves. Unable to keep his thoughts to himself, he turned to Declan and asked, "How did yer chieftain die?"

"A riding accident freed us from his yoke." Then he added quickly, "I ken 'tis not holy to speak ill of the dead, but there was little to recommend in Cormag Brodie's character."

"Was no one saddened by his passing?"

Declan shook his head grimly. "When they carried his lifeless body into the great hall, no one shed a tear—least of all, Elora."

"What of Elora's mother?"

Pain shadowed Declan's features. "Lady Moira died nearly eleven years ago when Elora was just ten and Temperance was five. Took ill with a fever, she did." He expelled a long breath. "She was only five and twenty, but despite her youth, she was frail...lovely but frail."

"Laird Brodie must have been hard on her."

Declan nodded. "He was a cruel husband."

"And demanding, no doubt."

But Declan shook his head sadly. "In a way, he was, but part of his cruelty was that he actually demanded very little of her. He gave her nothing but disdain. She had no say on any matter. She was trusted with no duties, allowed no purpose or interest. She could not even mother her daughters. He kept them apart, relying on wet nurses and castle servants to see to their needs."

"I'm surprised he did not remarry to beget an heir."

Declan lifted his shoulders. "Murray and I often wondered that very thing. We believe he never thought death would come for him." Then Declan winced. "I dread to think how he would have behaved toward a son. Laird Brodie did not share power."

"How did he treat Elora?"

"He took no interest in her; that is, until he realized he could marry her off as a means to gain greater wealth."

"She did not experience his cruelty firsthand?"

"Besides the occasional biting remark, he ignored her." Then Declan's face brightened. "But Elora worked this to everyone's advantage. Right beneath the blackguard's nose, she started making the rounds herself when she turned fifteen. Unbeknownst to her father, she would follow after him, healing all he harmed. She would sneak food to those in need. She raised their spirits and gained her people's trust. But she never let him see. She kept her work, her thoughts, her worries hidden from his cruel gaze."

Nathan slowly nodded. Now, he understood. For years, she had carried the wellbeing of the entire clan on her shoulders, but she had to do so in secret, doing what she must to hide her deeds from her father's watchful eye.

"Thank ye for trusting me enough to share yer lady's story," Nathan said. Then he raked his hand through his hair as his conscience pricked for not having given the captain the same trust. With a deep breath, he turned back and met the older man's gaze. "I did not leave my clan. I was banished by my father."

Brows drawn, Declan asked, "But why?"

A beautiful lass with black curls and startling blue eyes came to the fore of his mind. He shook the image from his thoughts. "Dark times befell our clan, for which my father blamed me."

"Was he right in his judgment?"

Nathan lifted his shoulders. "I suppose…at least, in part. Forgive me…I…" his words trailed off. He had never spoken of Cait to anyone, not even Caleb.

Declan gave him an assessing look, then he jerked his head toward the wagon. "Come, let us hitch up the horses. We've a few more stops to make today. Then we'll be back home by nightfall."

Home.

The word hung in the air around him. For the first time in a long time, he longed for home, for belonging, but then a mirthless laugh fled his lips as he jerked around and started up the shore toward the wagon.

The past could never be undone.

"Nathan," he stopped in his tracks and met Declan's gaze. "I was not in favor of my lady's plan when we set out for Edinburgh, but now I'm glad ye're here." The captain lifted his shoulders. "Sometimes things have a way of working out differently than we planned."

For the rest of the day, Declan's words stayed with him, and he wondered if he had truly accepted Lady Elora's offer because of a desire for greater wealth—after all, as Caleb had already pointed out, he had money to spare. What if his soul craved what he had long since believed he did not deserve?

When they arrived back at Castle Bròn, the moon shone brightly overhead. He sought out Elora's company straightaway. He knew not what he would say to her, only that he wanted desperately to see her. Murray, who had been meeting with several villagers in the courtyard when Declan drove the wagon through the open gates, directed Nathan to the solar.

Hastening through the great hall, he took the stairs onto the high dais two at a time. Once he passed behind the screen, he started down the passage toward the family rooms. Still several feet away from the solar, he drew to a halt when he heard upset voices emanating from the door, which was slightly ajar.

Quietly, so as to not be heard, he drew closer and listened.

"Days ago, ye said that we would go for a ride." He recognized Temperance's voice.

"I told ye. I've been busy," came Elora's clipped response.

"If ye're so busy that ye cannot stop to eat or take a short ride, why do ye not let me help ye?"

He leaned slightly forward to peer through the crack in the doorway and saw Elora shaking her head adamantly. "Ye don't have the skills."

"Nor will I unless ye teach me," Temperance shot back. "Elora, I spent another day alone in my chamber, embroidering, and then I wandered the castle aimlessly, because everyone else has a purpose except for me."

Elora studied the parchment on the table in front of her. "I'm sorry, but ye rush through tasks. Ye're never careful. Our people call ye Tempest lovingly, but also for a reason."

"Listen to yerself," Temperance said, her voice rising. "Ye're becoming just like him!"

Elora jerked upright. Nathan had never seen her eyes so cold. "Like whom?" she demanded.

"Like father!"

Elora's eyes flashed wide, then narrowed in anger. "I am nothing like him!"

Temperance shook her head. "Ye don't even see it," she said bitterly as she reached for something on the floor. "Here, ye dropped yer precious list."

Then she turned and crossed toward the door.

Nathan quickly retreated further down the hall, only to turn on his heel a moment later. Then he slowly walked back toward the solar to give the illusion that he had just arrived.

Temperance froze when she saw him, her eyes wide and flooded with tears. She opened her mouth to speak but only a sob came out. Covering her face with her hands, she stormed past him.

Hearing Elora's footfalls approaching the solar door, he again quickly retreated to the end of the hall, then turned back around and slowly walked back toward the solar so that she wouldn't know that he had overheard the altercation.

She stepped into the hallway, her face as impassive as ever, and stopped short when she saw him. Her fists suddenly unclenched. "Did ye enjoy yer ride?" she asked, her voice even.

"I did," he replied.

So many words clung to the tip of his tongue. He wanted to honor her courage and to comfort the pain he knew lived deep within her, but still she kept her shield of detachment in place.

She cleared her throat. "If ye'll excuse me, I'm going to retire to my chamber."

"Of course," he said, stepping out of her way. After she had strode past him, he called to her. "Elora."

She turned and met his gaze.

"Brodie land is beautiful, and yer people…they cherish ye."

"I know," she said simply. Then she turned back around.

He watched her go, wishing he could catch up to her and take her in his arms and tell her to let down her guard, smile, laugh—she had already won. But then the reality, which he had always known but never fully appreciated, suddenly rang true.

For Elora, the battle raged on. Without a husband, she was vulnerable and so were the good people of Clan Brodie.

Now, more than ever, he was determined to find a way to win her hand.

As he watched her near the end of the hallway, her feminine hips swaying as she glided, he was struck yet again by a new thought. Securing her hand was no longer enough.

He wanted to win her heart.

# Chapter Twelve

Elora began her morning as she always did. She broke her fast, made her list with Mary, dressed, and then she met with Murray in the solar. But after that, she did not tend to the first item scribbled on the small piece of parchment, which she had rolled into a slender cylinder and tucked under the cuff of her sleeve. Instead, she went in search of Temperance.

For so many years, Elora had been preoccupied with raising her people up that somehow along the way, she had let her sister down. She had neglected Temperance's education. Certainly, the task of taming her sister's impulsive whims had, in the past, felt overwhelming when coupled with her many other duties. Still, at ten and six, Temperance was no longer a child. Elora would just have to hone her own discipline to ensure she met the needs of everyone around her, including those of her sister.

The first place Elora looked for Temperance was her chamber, but the room was empty. She crossed to the table near the hearth and picked up her sister's needlework, which depicted waves crashing against rocks. In the exquisite detail, Elora could feel her sister's passion and restlessness. It stirred something in her own soul. She grazed her fingertips over the soft color, but then she shook her head and set the fabric down. Leaving the room, she continued her search.

On occasion, Temperance would help Agnes in the kitchen, especially when stewed apples were on the menu, but Temperance wasn't among the undercooks bustling around the tabletops. A prick of apprehension settled over Elora as she left the kitchen. Quickening her pace, she hastened out into the courtyard where she spied Declan who was hurrying her way. "My lady, I was just coming to find ye."

She held up her hand. "Whatever it is, it will have to wait. I'm looking for Temperance."

"She's in the fields beyond the stables, but, my lady, I really must—"

Her eyes flashed wide. "Ye let her ride alone?"

"Nay," he said quickly. "She's with Nathan and Caleb."

Elora picked up her skirts and hurried through the front gates. When she cleared the outer wall and had a view of the fields, she stopped in her tracks. Nathan was riding her sister's dappled gray mare, but he did not ride alone. Her skirts hitched high, Temperance sat astride her mount in front of him. Elora watched in horror as they charged at a stack of grain sacks.

"Nay!" she cried, rushing ahead.

"My lady, 'tis all right," she heard Declan call out.

Her breath caught as Temperance's horse bounded gracefully over the stack, drawing to a halt on the other side where Caleb awaited them astride his black mount.

Her face beaming, Temperance laughed with delight.

Elora shook her head at her sister's recklessness.

"My lady, she's all right," Declan said, catching up to her.

"Elora!" Temperance called when she saw her approach. Then Nathan turned the gray mare around and rode toward her.

"Elora, did ye see me?" Temperance asked, breathless, her face beaming with joy.

Elora swallowed her fury, fighting to keep her voice steady. "I see more of ye than I care to," she said looking pointedly at Temperance's bare calf.

Blushing, Temperance tugged at her hem, trying to pull it down. "I cannot learn to jump Hazel side-saddled, but Nathan said that once I master it sitting astride, then I can learn the proper way."

"Is that so?" Elora said, shifting her gaze to Nathan, but then her attention was drawn to his hand splayed wide on her sister's stomach. Her nostrils flared. She pressed her lips together, fighting for calm.

Caleb dismounted and crossed to her sister's mount. He reached up and grasped Temperance by the waist and lifted her down. "She's a skilled rider," Caleb added in a quiet voice.

Declan came forward then. "Exceptionally so."

Temperance nodded and her chin lifted with pride. "When they saw how well I could ride, Nathan suggested I learn to jump."

"Did he?" she said coldly, once more meeting Nathan's silver gaze.

He slid to the ground. "Elora—"

"Wait," she said, her voice clipped. Then she shifted her attention to the others. "I must speak with Nathan alone."

After Temperance, Caleb, and Declan were out of ear shot, she turned to Nathan. "She is a lady of Clan Brodie."

"I ken," he said, "but she is also a spirited lass."

"Do not praise her recklessness."

He raked his hand through his hair. "Listen to me, Elora. If ye want to keep the tempest at bay, ye need to give her more than needlework to occupy her time." A look of sudden anguish passed over his features. It was fleeting but unmistakable. "Trust me. I know of what I speak."

The truth of his words settled around her. "I ken," she said quietly. "I was planning on speaking with her about that very thing, but—"

"My lady!"

"What now?" she muttered, turning around to see the stable master rushing toward them on horseback. His rim of straggly black hair stood out on all sides while his bald head glinted in the morning sun.

Declan came forward then. "No doubt, Arthur wishes to discuss the matter I tried to address with ye in the courtyard. Laird Mackintosh has given ye a wedding present."

"A present?" she repeated. "Whatever did he send?"

"A horse," Declan answered. "But—"

The stable master thundered to a stop in front of them. Sweat beaded on his furrowed brow. "My lady, ye must come and quickly. I've had the lads searching the castle for ye."

"I'm coming, Arthur," she assured him and lifted the hem of her skirts, ready to race back to the castle, but then Nathan turned to her. "Ride with me."

She hesitated, but only for a moment. Reaching for his shoulders, he gripped her waist and lifted her onto the saddle before he swung up behind her. They galloped into the courtyard and followed Arthur straight into the stables. Caleb and Temperance joined them a moment later, riding in on his black steed.

Arthur slid from his horse and pointed at a sleek chestnut mare with a black mane, thrashing against the stall. She bucked and snorted, making the other horses sidestep nervously in their stalls.

Eyes wide, Elora asked, "She is our wedding present?"

"Make no mistake, my lady. She's no gift. The Devil resides in her soul. She'll not be ridden."

Temperance slid to the ground. "Don't say such things," she chided Arthur. "She's just scared." Slowly, Temperance started to approach the stall, but Caleb dismounted and quickly grasped her hand, shaking his head. "Nay," he said softly. "'Tis too dangerous."

"Thank ye, Caleb," Elora said.

Nathan slid from the dappled gray, then reached up and lifted Elora down.

"She'll not be ridden," Arthur repeated.

"Let me try," Temperance pleaded. "I know I can ride her. She just needs some gentle handling."

"Temperance, do ye even ken what ye're asking?" Elora said, shaking her head. Then she turned to one of the stable hands, standing off to the side. He was a young lad with ten and two years and thick brown hair, which he wore in a long braid down his back. "Jacob, please escort Temperance back to the castle."

Nodding, Jacob came forward, but Temperance's eyes became like sharp daggers that narrowed on her older sister. "He needn't bother. That's one thing that I'm perfectly capable of doing on my own."

Elora ignored her sister's displeasure and turned to Arthur. "What is yer judgment?"

"I believe 'tis a hidden insult. This beast will not be tamed. 'Tis a shame because she has good stock."

Elora shook her head. "I would expect nothing less from Egan." Then she declared. "No one rides her. Send her back."

"Wait," Nathan said, coming forward. "I will ride her."

She turned and met his expectant gaze. "Nay, 'tis too dangerous."

A smile curved his lips. "She's a beauty. The foals ye'll have from her stock will serve yer clan." He started to approach the horse, then he spied a door in the back of the stall. "Where does that gate lead?"

"Straight into the holding corral," Arthur replied. "Thankfully, we repaired the fence two days ago."

Nathan turned back to Elora. "What could be better than turning his insult into yer gain?"

Elora looked at the feral horse bucking and kicking while she considered Nathan's suggestion, but then she shook her head. "'Tis not worth the risk. Send her back."

Arthur nodded. "Aye, my lady," he said and dipped his head to her.

With the matter settled, she turned to leave.

"Elora," Nathan began, drawing her gaze, "forgive me," he said softly. His silver gaze held hers for several moments, but then he turned away and spoke to Arthur. "Go around to the holding corral. When ye hear me give the word, open the gate."

Arthur nodded. "Come on, Jacob," he said, motioning to the lad.

Elora watched in surprise as Arthur obeyed Nathan's command and left the stables. He hadn't even sought her approval first. She turned to reprimand Nathan for using his temporary status to take the upper hand, but she faltered as she watched him climb up on the side of the stall.

"Nathan, this is lunacy!"

He looked at her and she saw a glint in his eyes—wild and dangerous. It was the same glint she had witnessed at The Devil's Bridge.

"We're not going to allow Egan to win this battle."

She shook her head. "'Tis not worth it!"

A slow sideways smile curved his lips. "Trust me." Then he turned back to the mare. He stood there for some time, crooning soft words, touching her coat when she came close enough. Still, the beast kicked and snorted. Finally, Nathan called out. "Arthur are ye ready?"

"Aye, my laird," Arthur answered from the other side of the gate.

Elora's eyes flashed wide when she heard her stable master's reply.

"Get back," Caleb said, clasping her hand and pulling her away from the stall.

In a flash, Nathan leapt onto the mare's back, seizing fistfuls of her mane. "Now," he shouted. The gate behind the stall swung open, and the mare bolted outside.

"Come, my lady," Caleb urged her, pulling her from the stables into the courtyard. Together, they raced to the holding corral where Nathan fought to stay on the mare's back while she bucked and kicked and tossed her neck.

Elora gripped the fence. "He's going to get himself killed!"

Caleb expelled a long breath "I'm not sure that's not his ultimate goal," he said quietly.

She turned to face him. "What do ye mean?"

He shook his head. "'Tis nothing."

"Tell me," she insisted.

He lifted his shoulders. "Ye were at The Devil's Bridge. Ye saw him attack the giant, Bowie."

She nodded.

"He knew I was on my way. What's more, he left his sword behind."

Brow's drawn, she asked. "What are ye trying to say?"

Caleb shook his head. "I do not ken. There is much to Nathan that is still unknown to me, despite the years we've worked together. He is haunted. That much I do know, but by what I cannot say."

She gasped as Nathan was thrown from the wild mare's back. "Enough," she shouted.

But he leapt to his feet and chased after the mare. Seizing her mane, he swung up on her back.

"If anyone can tame her, 'tis Nathan," Caleb assured her.

"Not if she breaks him first," she muttered. Then she jerked around. "I cannot watch!"

"My lady, allow me to escort ye to the castle," Caleb offered. "This will take a while."

She shook her head, showing her back to the corral. "Nay, just tell me if he is injured."

What felt like hours passed. She chewed her lip and paced back and forth, glancing every now and then at Nathan to be sure he was still alive.

The horse snorted, drawing her gaze. She turned just as Nathan was thrown to the ground again.

"Please, make him stop," she pleaded to Caleb and looked away.

"My lady," Caleb said, once more drawing her gaze. "Look!"

She turned toward the corral and clutched the fence while she watched Nathan slowly walk toward the mare whose head hung low with fatigue. As he closed in on her, Elora could hear him speaking gently to the mare. When he reached the horse's side, he slowly stroked his hand down her neck. She jerked upright and skittered back, but she did not stomp or kick. Then Nathan swung up on her back again. She snorted and stomped at the ground, but she did not buck. He nudged her forward, and she took several steps. Leaning low, keeping his body close to the mare, he continued to stroke her neck and croon soft praises.

Elora's heart raced as Nathan and the mare drew closer. She expected him to gloat, or for him at least to look triumphant. But when he smiled at her, she was struck by the hollowness she glimpsed in his eyes. In that moment, she realized what had always made Nathan's gaze so compelling. She was drawn to the quiet plea in his eyes. As she continued to watch him, her chest tightened.

"My lady," Arthur called.

She tore her gaze from Nathan's as the stable master rushed toward her with Jacob following just behind. "I am astonished! I've never seen such skillful riding!"

Elora took a deep breath and straightened her back, suppressing the well of emotion flooding her heart. She allowed a pleasant smile to upturn her lips. "It would appear that we are able to keep the mare after all," she said.

Arthur nodded. "It will be a few days before we'll be able to get a bridle and saddle on her, and several weeks longer until she'll be safe for others to ride. But what impressed me most is that yer betrothed used gentleness and persistence to bring her around when some men might have resorted to the brutality of the whip." He smiled, his eyes crinkling at the sides. "Ye've chosen a mate wisely, my lady. He is kind. I do not doubt that ye'll be very happy together."

Happy.

She had never given much thought to being happy. Her life had always been about duty and survival.

Her gaze shifted back to Nathan. His thighs flexed as he

squeezed the mare between his legs and continued to trot around the corral. Then her breath caught as he released the mare's mane. His back arched, and he stretched his arms out to the side and let his head fall back. His eyes closed as if he was surrendering himself up to the sky. She leaned against the fence, compelled by what she saw. She knew all too well what he was feeling, for the same hole made her own heart impossible to fill.

# Chapter Thirteen

*N*athan sat huddled in the corner deep within the belly of a ship, rocking back and forth while great swells crashed, and thunder rumbled. Water leaked through cracks in the deck, soaking him. He heard the cries of sailors fighting the storm and the ship creaking against the might of the angry sea.

"Nathan," a soft voice said.

*He jerked around. There, in the opposite corner, was a lass with her legs curled up to her chest and fear blazing in her blue eyes. Her wet black curls clung to her ashen face.*

*"Nathan, I'm afraid. I don't want to die."*

Nathan sat up with a start. Sweat dripped from his temples. His breaths came in short bursts. He swept his blanket off and swung his legs over the side of the bed and cradled his pounding head in his hands. Cait's plea still echoed in his mind.

"I'm sorry," he whispered. "I'm so very sorry."

He couldn't escape his dream. Standing, he seized his plaid and belted it around his hips, leaving the upper folds to hang from his waist. Then he crossed his chamber floor and slowly opened his door enough to peer out. Torch fire, set in sconces along the hallway walls, cast dancing shadows on the ceiling. He listened intently, but no one stirred.

Stepping from his chamber, he eased the door shut behind him. Then, he quietly made his way down to the great hall where he spied several servants asleep on pallets laid out near the hearth. Softly padding barefoot across the cold stone floor, he entered the kitchen and headed straight for the buttery where he claimed a flagon of wine. Hooking his finger through the ring at the neck, he brought the vessel to his lips, taking a long draught. He closed his eyes, savoring the rich flavor, and expelled a long breath. With the flagon still hooked on his finger, he returned to the great hall and sat in a high-backed chair just to the side of the hearth.

His gaze passed over the servants who were still fast asleep. Then he shifted his gaze to the fire, which hissed and crackled, the flames dancing wildly. After several more draughts of wine, he laid his head back and closed his eyes. No longer did raven-black curls and blue eyes fill his mind. Nor could he hear his father's voice raised in anger, telling him to be gone from his sight, to leave Campbell lands and never return.

The familiar numbness had begun to set in.

He was about to drift back to sleep when something wet nudged his hand. He opened his eyes and met the gaze of a dog with floppy ears, short gray hair, and beseeching yellow eyes.

Nathan scratched behind the animal's ear. "Thank ye, my friend," he whispered. "It wouldn't do for Elora to find me here on the morrow."

He stood up and motioned for the dog to follow him into the kitchen. In the pantry, he found some cooked ribs and offered one to his furry companion who snatched it out of his hand, then dashed to the far side of the room and began to gnaw on his prize.

Nathan lifted the flagon to toast the dog and brought it to

his lips, letting the rich liquid course down his throat before he once more entered the great hall. With care to not awaken the servants, he crossed to the high dais, then moved behind the screen. Once in the hallway, he noticed that the solar door was slightly ajar. The soft glow of candlelight emanating from the room beckoned him closer.

He peered inside. Brows drawn, Elora stood in front of her table, shuffling frantically through pieces of parchment. She was clad in a simple linen nightgown with lace trim around the collar and sleeves. Her unbound golden hair glinted in the candlelight. Crumpling the pages suddenly in her hands, she dropped them on the table.

"I didn't think anyone else was awake," he said softly.

She sucked in a sharp breath and looked up. They locked eyes.

Slowly, holding her gaze, he walked around the table to stand beside her. With his free hand, he reached out and gently grazed his fingers down her cheek. Her eyes squeezed shut and her breath caught. Her tongue darted out, licking her tremulous full lips. "Nathan," she breathed, her voice a whispered plea.

Dear God above but he wanted her.

He had never seen her so raw, so vulnerable. He knew in that moment that he could have her. She wouldn't resist if he were to take her hand and lead her to his bed.

He could make her his wife.

But he would never take advantage of her desperation, nor did he wish to seduce her at all. He wanted her to come to him of her own free will.

He searched her eyes. "Tell me something, Elora," he began, his voice whisper-soft. "What do ye really want?"

Tears flooded her eyes. She pressed her lips together in a

109

grim line, fighting back the swell of emotion he knew ached to break free. She shook her head. A single tear coursed down her cheek. "I...I do not know." Her voice cracked.

"Neither do I," he replied softly.

Pain emanated from her gaze, mirroring his own broken heart. But he drew strength from their sameness. Hooked on his finger, he raised the wine vessel he held for her to see. "But I do know one thing—I'm not going to find the answer at the bottom of this flagon." Then he looked pointedly at her parchment strewn table. "And yer lists will not help ye either." His nostrils flared as he set the flagon down on the table and took a step back, distancing himself from the bottle.

Steeling his shoulders, he took another deep breath, forcing his mind to clear. Then he held out his hand to her. "Come with me, Elora. I will walk ye to yer chamber."

She swallowed hard. "Nay, I...I can't." Her hands fluttered, smoothing out the crumpled pages, her gaze darting over their surfaces. "I'm running out of time."

"Elora," he said again, his voice gently persuasive. "Come with me."

Once more their eyes locked. She dropped the page and slid her hand into his. Then he slowly led her toward the door. Stepping into the hallway, he pulled her close to his side and wrapped his arm around her waist. Her body softened. She rested her head against his shoulder, her hand splayed wide on his chest as they walked.

A comfortable silence hung in the air, surrounding them.

When they reached her chamber door, he opened it and let his hand drop from her waist.

"Goodnight, Elora," he said softly.

She turned to him. "Thank ye, Nathan."

With a dip of his head, he took another step back, but then she seized his hand.

"Ye're smile never touches yer eyes," she blurted.

Sucking in a sharp breath, he drew close and cupped her cheek. "And yers never sees the light of day." He longed to hold her, to comfort her, but with a deep breath he stepped back and started to turn away.

"Nathan," she said.

"Aye, my lady," he answered softly.

Building slowly at first, a smile spread across her face, the first she had ever given him.

His chest tightened at the sight. He dipped his head in gratitude.

Then she slowly shut her door, her gaze locked with his until it closed.

He pressed his palm against the wood, fighting the urge to throw open the door, take her in his arms and kiss away all her hurt, making her his wife in name and body.

Backing away, he slowly retreated to his room with her full smile filling his mind's eye. And for the first time that he could remember, he smiled and knew that it was real. And had she been there, she would have seen that it, indeed, reached his eyes.

# Chapter Fourteen

**M**ary stood by the kitchen stairs that led to the chamber rooms, waiting for the chapel bell to toll for *Lauds*. When the first chime rang out, she turned and looked intently at the breakfast tray to make sure it met with her lady's meticulous standards. Using the corner of her apron to wipe away a few scattered crumbs, Mary nodded her approval, took up the tray, and started her ascent to her lady's chamber. With a steady, practiced hand, she swept down the hallway, then knocked softly on her lady's door, and waited for her customary reply.

But it never came.

Brows drawn, Mary puzzled for a moment. She had never needed to knock twice, but then again, her lady had seemed out of sorts the previous eventide when she had helped her dress for bed. Mayhap she did not sleep well. Mary chewed her lip and considered whether she should let Lady Elora sleep longer, but then she shook her head. Maintaining a schedule was especially important to her ladyship.

Confident she was doing her duty, Mary rapped her knuckles against the door, only this time she knocked harder. But, once again, she heard no reply.

Now, all manner of nightmarish thoughts coursed through the young maid's mind. What if her lady had been kidnapped in the night? Or mayhap, Laird Mackintosh had scaled the castle wall and smothered Lady Elora in her sleep. Heart racing, Mary knocked again. Still, no answer.

Steeling her heart against the worst, Mary balanced the tray on one arm and threw open the door. Her gaze went first to the bed, but it was empty. Then she scanned the room.

"My lady," she exclaimed, seeing her leaning out the casement clad in naught but her kirtle. But Lady Elora did not turn around.

Mary set the tray on its customary table, then hastened to the window and gently touched her lady's arm. She jumped a little before she straightened and turned to face her maid.

"What is it, Mary?"

Confused, Mary asked, "My lady, did ye not hear me?"

Lady Elora's brow wrinkled. "I'm sorry, Mary, did ye say something?"

Mary's gaze darted to her lady, then the door, then to the tray on the table. "Nay...I mean, aye...I mean, I was knocking...'tis *Lauds*, my lady. I have yer breakfast tray."

Lady Elora shook her head. "Thank ye but not today. I would like to get an early start."

Mary's mouth fell open as her lady padded barefoot across the floor to her wardrobe, which she threw open. "This will do," she said, seizing a pale blue tunic, which she pulled over her head.

"Do not look so surprised, Mary. Ye don't suppose Declan helped me dress all the while we were away?"

"Nay, my lady, of course not. I...er..." but Mary did not know how to reply.

Lady Elora slid her feet into a pair of slippers and turned toward the door. "Come along then."

"But, my lady, yer hair!"

Lady Elora paused and smoothed her hands over her unbound flaxen curls. "'Tis fine," she said. "Now, come along."

"What of yer surcote and…and…yer list!"

"No time," came her lady's quick reply.

Mary stood frozen in place for a moment as her lady disappeared out the door without adornment or refinement of any kind, and, most importantly, without a list. When her shock wore off, leaving her stomach doing somersaults, Mary followed after.

On any typical day, Lady Elora would have taken the main stairs to the family rooms, where, doubtless, at that very moment, Murray was awaiting her in the solar.

But Mary was beginning to realize that there was nothing typical about the day.

She followed her ladyship to the servants' stairwell. Before too long, Mary was back in the kitchen where Lady Elora was speaking with Agnes. The rest of the servants were bustling about, casting curious looks her way.

Her ladyship set her hands at her hips. "I am going to reorganize the kitchen today."

Agnes's eyes flashed wide. "The whole kitchen!"

The cook shot Mary a questioning look, but Mary could only lift her shoulders.

Agnes cleared her throat. "Of course, if ye say so, my lady." Then her eyes brightened. "Why don't ye start with the pantry. Ye will find Allison already hard at work. In fact…" Agnes gave Mary a pointed look. "Mary, why don't ye go and fetch her now and see if she can *help* our lady."

Mary nodded quickly and rushed to the pantry. Allison was sitting on an overturned barrel with a basket of eggs at her feet. "Please come quickly," Mary began, "Our ladyship needs ye."

Allison grimaced as she started to stand. "I'm afraid there is little I can do quickly these days, except for tiring out."

Mary dashed back to the kitchen. She was grateful to see that Agnes had dismissed the other servants. "Allison is coming."

When the pantler shuffled into the kitchen, Agnes motioned to where her ladyship was pulling pots down from a shelf.

"Good morrow, my lady," Allison said brightly.

Lady Elora turned. "Good morrow."

Mary watched Allison's expression alter as she took in her lady's less than polished appearance. "Ye're...er...looking well this morrow."

Lady Elora set down the pot she held and crossed to Allison's side and placed her hand on the pantler's swollen stomach. "As are ye. Ye're time draws near."

Allison smiled. "Aye, my lady." Then her face lit up. "Soon, it will be yer turn."

Lady Elora's eyes flashed wide with alarm. "What?" Her gaze darted around the room as if she had lost something. "What...is that on the floor?" she suddenly exclaimed.

Wringing her hands, Mary followed behind as her lady hastened to the corner of the kitchen. "What is it, my lady?"

Brow furrowed, Lady Elora grimaced at a smear on the stone floor. "'Tis some kind of dried sauce."

"I will clean it," Mary said, rushing over to a bucket and seizing a rag. But when she returned, her ladyship took the rag from her hand.

"I will tend to it myself."

Mary, Allison, and Agnes gasped simultaneously.

Helpless, Mary wrung her hands as her lady dropped to her knees and began scrubbing at the spill.

"Please, my lady," Agnes pleaded. "Ye mustn't. It simply isn't proper."

Mary whirled around and locked eyes with the cook. "I'm going for help."

~ * ~

Nathan sat beside Declan and Caleb at the high table. While the other men discussed Declan's training exercises that he planned to lead the warriors through after they broke their fast, Nathan had thoughts only for Elora. He closed his eyes and remembered every detail from the night before—the way her unbound curls shimmered in the candlelight; the creamy expanse of her neck revealed by the cut of her nightgown. But more than anything, his mind fixated on the emotion in her eyes and in her breath and touch—fear, longing, hope—he had felt it all, emanating from her very soul.

He pushed aside his half-eaten bannock and turned to give his excuses to Declan when he noticed Mary moving toward the high dais. His eyes narrowed on Elora's maid whose stiff gait and strained smile were uncharacteristic for the slender lass who typically moved like a wee bird, darting from room to room. When they locked eyes, he could see the worry in her gaze, although he could tell she fought to conceal her feelings.

"Excuse me," he said to Declan. Then he crossed the dais and walked casually down the stairs.

"My laird," Mary began in a hushed voice when he crossed to her side.

"Call me Nathan," he said, interrupting her. Then his lips

curved in a slight smile. "Yer lady and I are not married yet."

"Nathan," Mary said, correcting herself. "We have need of yer presence in the kitchen."

He was surprised by Mary's request. "Whatever it is, I'm sure our lady is the one to ask. She needn't any help when it comes to the smooth running of Castle Bròn."

"On the contrary," Mary hissed. "My lady is in great need of yer help."

He stiffened. "Lead on then."

He followed the maid into the kitchen. Straightaway, he noticed the stricken looks on the cook's and pantler's faces, but Elora was nowhere to be seen. "Where is she?"

Mary pointed to the far side of the room.

If he didn't know better, he would have assumed that one of the village lassies was helping Agnes. But the long, blonde curls were undeniable. Elora was on her hands and knees scrubbing at the floor in a frenzy.

He drew close, and he cleared his throat. "Ye missed a spot in the corner."

~ * ~

Elora jerked upright on her knees. "Oh, tis ye!" Her face burned as she met his curious gaze. Heart pounding, palms sweating, she cleared her throat, clutching the rag in her fist. "What can I help ye with?" She tilted her chin, trying to muster as much dignity as she could. "As ye can see I'm terribly busy." Unable to withstand the tenderness of his smoldering gaze, she looked away and renewed her scrubbing. It was a battle she was determined to win. She would rid the floor of the dried spill just as she would rid her mind and heart of all thoughts pertaining

117

to hired renegades whose insights into her soul could penetrate all her defenses.

"Elora." His voice called to her as soft as a caress.

"What?" she snapped, looking up. He had drawn closer, standing directly above her.

Her stomach fluttered.

He squatted down so that they were eye level "Ye don't quite seem like yerself today."

Her pulse raced. She brushed at the dirt on her tunic. "Whatever do ye mean?"

His gaze trailed over her slowly. She felt it like a touchless caress. "Ye're not wearing a surcote." He reached out and gently grasped a lock of her hair. "And yer beautiful hair is unbound and trailing on the floor."

She swallowed hard. "One does not wear their best clothes to clean the kitchen."

A playful smile upturned one corner of his mouth. "When one is a lady, she typically does not scrub the floor."

Agnes cleared her throat. "He does make a very good point, my lady."

Elora looked beyond Nathan to where Agnes, Mary, and Allison stood, each woman wearing a look of confused concern on her face. "One clan, one back," Elora answered stiffly.

She knew she was not behaving like herself, but she was not to blame.

She turned an accusing gaze at the ridiculously gorgeous man whose face was now a breath from her own. Jumping to her feet. She dusted her hands off. "I'm fine, everyone. Spring is nigh upon us. I simply wanted to make sure the kitchen was ready for the new season, and that was when I noticed this spill."

He stood, and, once again, they were only a breath apart. "Ye and I both know that ye didn't get much sleep last night," he said softly.

He reached for her hand, but she snatched it away. "I'm dirty. Ye do not want to touch me."

"On the contrary," he began, a seductive smile curving his lips as he gently took her hand in his.

Her mouth went dry. She licked her lips. Her heart raced.

"Ladies, will ye excuse us for just a moment," Nathan said, his intense gaze never leaving hers

"Nay!" she exclaimed, snatching her hand away again. Then she shifted her gaze toward the women who had turned on their heels to leave the room. "Please don't go." She clutched her hands together to cease their shaking. "I can see that I've caused some alarm with my informal dress. I will just take my leave then and remedy my appearance."

Nathan clasped her waist as she brushed past him. "Allow me to walk ye to yer chamber."

"Nay," she blurted, her heart pounding harder than ever. She seriously doubted whether she would have the self-discipline to leave him outside her chamber door. The image of her throwing her arms around his neck and kissing him the way she had wanted to so desperately the night before came unbidden to her mind. "I'm quite capable of finding my chamber," she said quickly.

A sensual smile tugged at Nathan's lips as if he could read her very thoughts. "Ye really are quite dirty," he said, his voice husky. "Mayhap ye might allow me to order ye a bath."

Visions of him kneeling next to her bathtub, running a wet cloth along her bare thigh assaulted her mind. But just when she could not take his penetrating stare another moment, Firtha, Temperance's high-strung maid, came racing into the kitchen, her brow drawn with worry. "My lady, ye must come!"

"I'm coming," Elora blurted with relief, but she faltered when she noticed the tears flooding Firtha's eyes.

She grabbed her sister's maid by the arms. "What has happened?"

"Temperance is in the field beyond the stables. She—"

Elora did not stay to listen to Firtha's explanation. Instead, she hitched her tunic up and set out at a run. In a flash, Nathan was at her side. Together, they raced out into the courtyard just as Declan was leading a charge of warriors out of the stables.

"My lady," Declan said, drawing his mount to a halt next to her. Before she knew what was happening, Nathan was lifting her onto the saddle behind her guard. Then Declan kicked his mount in the flanks, and they charged forward. Glancing back, she saw Nathan swing up behind Caleb whose black steed raced ahead, passing Declan and the other warriors.

"What has she done now?" Elora shouted for Declan to hear.

"Firtha came racing through the gates moments ago, claiming that Tempest was trying to ride the new horse."

Elora's chest tightened. "Not the one from Egan?"

"Aye, my lady, the same."

Her stomach dropped out. "God have mercy," she prayed.

They rounded the outer wall. Caleb had reined in his horse. Declan brought his mount alongside and signaled for the other riders to stop. Elora shifted her gaze beyond to the distant field, and it was then she saw her sister. "Nay," she cried as she watched Temperance holding fast to the horse's black mane while the beast bucked and kicked.

"Ride!" she bade Declan.

"Nay," Caleb snapped, his face drawn with worry. "If we charge toward her, it will spook the mare even more."

Nathan reached over from where he sat behind Caleb and squeezed her hand. "Wait here with Declan. We will save her."

Fear pulsed through her, choking her words. She nodded and Caleb nudged his mount forward at a gentle trot.

"Nathan," she called.

He looked back.

"She's all I have."

He held her gaze, his jaw set firm. Then he turned back around.

"Fear not, my lady. Nathan and Caleb will save her," Declan said, but she could hear the fear in his voice.

Fists clenched, she watched her sister struggle to keep her seat. "Don't give up, Temperance!" Barely breathing, not daring to blink, she prayed under her breath and kept her gaze fixed on the distant field.

Straightening in her seat, she could see that the chestnut horse had ceased her bucking and was now stomping at the ground, thrashing her head from side to side. She reared up on her hind legs. Temperance held her grip. Then suddenly, her sister was galloping across the field, bent low on the horse's back.

Tears flooded Elora's eyes. "She's doing it! She's riding her!" Laughter bubbled up her throat. "Declan, she's riding her!"

"Would ye look at that," her guard said with a tone of wonderment in his voice.

Ahead of them, she saw Caleb draw up on his reins. His black mount shuffled in place as Nathan and Caleb both watched. Nathan turned around and waved back at her, a smile shaping his features. Then she shifted her gaze back to her younger sister who was riding the horse as if they were one and the same—like a schooner sailing across the open seas.

Temperance reached the end of the field and spun her mount

around, charging back the way she'd come, her black curls fanning out behind her.

Elora's heart swelled with pride. "She's amazing!" She watched in wonder at the skill with which Temperance managed the headstrong mare. In that moment, she was struck by how blind she had been to her sister's gifts. Temperance wasn't simply reckless—she was fearless. She was strong, and she had grown into a remarkable woman.

She squeezed Declan around the waist. "Look at her! Look at how she rides. I bet not a warrior in yer charge could ride so well."

"I dare say ye're right, my lady!"

Suddenly, a covey of grouse shot up in Temperance's path, the birds flying off in every direction. Elora sucked in a sharp breath as the wild mare reared up on her hind legs, tossing Temperance to the ground.

"Get up," Elora cried, but her sister lay unmoving while the horse bucked and kicked, narrowly missing her.

"She'll be crushed!"

"Look!" Declan shouted, pointing at Caleb and Nathan who had charged ahead.

When they reached her sister, Caleb slid from his mount, gathered Temperance up in his arms, and dashed away to safety while Nathan took the reins and chased after the spooked mare.

"Ride, Declan!"

They charged forward, and when they drew close to where Caleb was sitting with Temperance lying in his arms, Declan drew his mount to a halt. Elora slid to the ground and dropped to her knees beside her sister.

"Temperance," she cried and gasped when she saw blood oozing down her sister's cheek.

"She's alive," Caleb said, holding Temperance close. "But she has a nasty gash on her head."

Summoning her strength, Elora took a deep breath and stood. She turned to Declan. "Ride to the village and fetch the midwife." Then she turned to Caleb. "We must get her back to the castle."

He cradled Temperance in his arms and stood. "I will carry her."

Her heart pounding, fists clenched, Elora watched Declan race off toward the village while Caleb carried her unconscious sister toward the castle. Fear pulsed through her, assaulting her defenses. She fought for calm, for breath. But something fierce brewed within her, tumultuous and demanding. She pressed her hand against her mouth as a well of emotion threatened to choke the very breath from her body.

"Elora!"

Her chest hitched. Nathan raced toward her with the wild mare in tow.

"Elora!"

She started to run to him. When he drew close, he slid to the ground.

"Nathan," she cried, racing into his open arms. A sob tore from her throat as she threw her arms around his neck. He crushed her close.

"I've got ye," he crooned, and her control shattered.

She pressed her face into his neck. Her tears fell freely. It all poured out of her—her fear for her sister's life, the weight of caring for her people, Egan's claim, her indecision, and her newest fear…the fear that she was losing her heart to the very man who now held her in his arms, crooning soft promises that everything was going to be all right.

# Chapter Fifteen

Elora sat on the edge of her sister's bed, waiting for Temperance to at last open her eyes. The midwife had dressed her wound. Layers of linen were now wrapped securely around Temperance's head, taming her raven-black hair. Elora reached out and touched one of her sister's curls. Elora's flaxen hair had come from her father, but Temperance took after their mother in appearance—dark hair, fair skin, and blue eyes, although their mother's eyes had never shone with the same fire that burned in Temperance's bright gaze. The only thing her mother's eyes had ever held was suffering.

Elora stroked her fingertips down her sister's pale cheek. She looked so innocent and fragile, lying in the center of her four-poster bed with the blanket pulled up to her chin. For a moment, Elora felt as if she were a child again. She closed her eyes against the memory that rushed to the fore of her mind of another time she had kept vigil at a Brodie woman's bedside. Elora had only been ten when her mother died, but she would never forget her mother's gaunt cheeks or desperate eyes or the promise Elora had made her mother on the very day she drew her last breath.

Temperance's eyelashes fluttered, drawing Elora back into the present.

Holding her breath, she leaned close, waiting, watching. Then her sister stirred and slowly opened her eyes.

"Elora," she whispered, her voice hoarse.

Tears stung Elora's eyes. "Ye gave me such a fright."

Temperance's smiled faltered. "I ken ye're going to tell me how foolish I am."

Elora leaned close, cupping her sister's cheeks. "Nay, sweetling. 'Tis I who have been the fool."

Her sister's brows drew together. "Ye're not going to scold me for riding Storm?"

Laughing softly through her tears, Elora asked, "Is that the wee beastie's name then?"

With a look of incredulity in her eyes, Temperance nodded.

Elora took a deep breath. "I'm not going to scold ye. On the contrary, I was going to tell ye that ye were brilliant."

Temperance's blue eyes flashed wide, and then they flooded with tears. "Truly? I...I cannot remember the last time ye gave me any praise."

Elora pressed her lips together against the rush of emotion that surged up her throat. "Neither can I," she admitted. Then she climbed under the covers and held her sister close. "I am so very sorry." Wet tears coursed down her cheeks. "I've been so blind. Ye were right when ye said I was becoming like da."

Temperance pulled away and looked at her with pleading eyes. "Nay, Elora! I never should have said that. I've been selfish, thinking only of myself while ye carry the weight of our entire clan on yer shoulders."

Taking a deep breath, Elora swiped at her eyes. "A weight I need not carry alone. Clan Brodie has two ladies."

Her sister's eyes brightened. "What are ye saying?"

Elora smiled. "When ye're feeling better, we'll discuss yer

125

new duties."

Temperance clasped her hands together. "Like what?"

"Like helping Agnes with the menu." Elora chuckled. "I imagine stewed apples will be a common occurrence."

Temperance wrapped her arms around Elora's neck. "Thank ye!"

Elora savored the moment of closeness. Then she drew away and cupped her sister's cheek. "Keep riding if it brings ye joy."

"Truly? I may ride Storm again?"

"Of course, ye can. She's yers."

"Ye're giving her to me?"

Elora nodded. Then she took a deep breath and looked her sister hard in the eye. "I have underestimated ye. I'll never do it again."

A fresh rush of tears filled Temperance's eyes. "I love ye, Elora."

She pulled her sister close, once more. "And I love ye… Tempest."

The sister's talked quietly for a while longer as Tempest peppered Elora with questions about her new duties. But after a while, Tempest's eyes began to droop.

Elora pressed a kiss to her brow. "Ye rest now, sweetling. Ye'll need yer strength to complete the lists I'm going to give ye."

A sleepy smile curved Tempest's lip. "My own list," she said dreamily. Then her eyes closed.

Elora crossed the room and lifted the handle on her sister's door when suddenly Tempest said, "My joy is riding. What's yers?"

Elora's smile faltered. "I…I do not ken." She forced her smile to return. "Mayhap ye will help me find mine."

Tempest nodded and closed her eyes again. "Make that the first item on my list."

Elora stepped out into the hallway and shut the door. She leaned her head back against the wall and closed her eyes.

"How is she?"

She opened her eyes and turned, meeting Caleb's worried gaze. "She is well, tired, but well. She is resting now, but later if ye wish to visit her, ye—"

"Nay," he said quickly. "I just wanted to know that she was all right." He dipped his head. "I will take my leave." Then he turned on his heel and marched down the hall.

Nathan came forward then. "I'm certain Tempest is not the only one in need of rest."

She nodded. "How did ye know?"

He smiled gently. "Ye started out this day on yer hands and knees scrubbing the kitchen floor. By now, I can only imagine how tired ye must be." He wrapped his arm around her waist. "Come, I will walk ye to yer chamber."

When they reached her door, he opened it, then stepped back. "There was something I promised ye earlier." A slight smile curved one side of his mouth. "'Tis waiting for ye." He took her hand and turned it over and pressed his firm, sensual mouth to her palm. Then he straightened, and his silver eyes locked with hers as he backed away.

She watched his retreat, her stomach fluttering and her heart racing. Finally, she forced herself to enter her room. Straightaway, her gaze fell on the tub near the hearth. Coils of steam rose from the surface of the water. When she saw his thoughtfulness, her chest tightened. She stood frozen as gratitude and affection made her heart swell. Her breath caught. She threw open her door.

"Nathan!" she shouted after him.

He stopped and turned around.

Hitching up her tunic, she raced down the hallway and threw herself into his arms. He lifted her feet off the ground. His mouth covered hers. Hungrily, he coaxed her lips open with his tongue. She trembled with passion. Like a savage dance, their tongues intertwined, delving, stroking, sending shockwaves of ecstasy to her very core which burned with a need that ached soul-deep. She clung to him, wishing they could be closer still. The pain, sweet and agonizing, grew, taking her higher and higher until she feared she would either be saved, or she would erupt into flames and lose herself forever.

"Nay," she cried, thrusting him away.

He stumbled back, his chest heaving.

"Go!" she bade him.

Shaking his head, he closed the distance between them and reached for her, but she shook her head, retreating out of reach. "I can take no more," she cried.

He raked his hand through his hair. "Elora!"

"Please, Nathan. I am begging ye. Just go!"

His nostrils flared. His silver eyes burned with passion. But he blew out a long stream of air and backed away. Without another word, he turned on his heel and walked away from her. She raced back to her room and crumpled to the floor, burying her face in her knees.

"What have I done?" she sobbed. For she knew her soul had found its match, but love was for anyone else, not her. Her fate had been decided on the very day she first drew breath. She was Lady Elora Brodie, and her heart belonged to her clan.

# Chapter Sixteen

Nathan sat at the high table with Caleb on one side, but the chair to his left sat empty. Elora had yet to come down for supper. He closed his eyes and for a moment he was back in the hallway, his heart pounding as she raced toward him. Crushing her to him, he had claimed her lips in an explosive kiss that even in remembrance made his pulse race. She had clung to him, her mouth devouring, meeting the demand of his lips with a hunger all her own. She had given herself fully to the passion he had always known burned deep beneath her stony façade; that is, until she had pushed him away.

Movement out of the corner of his eye drew his attention back to the present. Caleb was gesturing to one of the serving lasses who was holding a flagon of wine. She nodded when she noticed Caleb motioning to her and hastened up the steps to the high dais to fill his cup.

Nathan leaned close. "Is that yer third tankard?"

Caleb raised a brow at him and leaned back in his chair. "Are ye going to chide me about my cups?"

Nathan shifted in his seat and looked at his friend straight on. "How is it that ye're drinking, and I'm not?"

"Because like ye, I have a woman on my mind, but unlike ye, I want to forget mine."

Nathan raised his brows, then called out to the serving lass on her way back down the stairs to the main floor. "Don't go far. He'll need another."

She tossed her unbound flaxen hair off her shoulder and flashed Caleb a suggestive smile. "I'll stay close, very close."

Caleb grunted into his cup. "Just what I need, another woman." Then he turned to Nathan. "Remind me again what exactly we're doing here?"

"Funny ye should ask that," Nathan said thoughtfully. "If ye recall, I came here to be laird. Now…" He shook his head. "Now, there's only one thing I want."

Caleb took a sip, then raised a brow at him. "Ye've lost yer heart, haven't ye?" he said knowingly.

Nathan shook his head. "Nay, my friend, I've found it. For the first time in years, I feel it pounding in my chest," he said, emphasizing each word with a strike of his fist to his chest. "What's more, I've found the woman I want to give my heart to."

A lazy sideways smile shaped Caleb's mouth as he sat back in his chair. "Do ye mean the uptight noblewoman ye've saddled yerself with?"

Nathan raised a brow at his friend. "Are ye throwing my words back at me?"

"I'm just reminding ye that I was opposed to this mission from the start and for good reason. Look at us. Ye're mooning like a lovesick lass, and I'm about to call that lassie with the wine back over so that she can fill my cup for the fourth time."

"Mayhap, ye shouldn't drown yer heart in wine," Nathan offered. "Why do ye not just tell Tempest how ye feel?"

Caleb frowned. "What makes ye think I've got that wee lassie on my mind?"

"I have eyes, don't I?" Nathan shot back. "Oh, and by the by, she isn't such a wee lassie."

Caleb stood, shaking his head. "Do ye ken what I think, Nathan?" he drawled. "I think I liked ye better when ye were broken and cynical."

Nathan chuckled. "Where are ye going, ye drunken sod?"

"To the stables where I don't have to listen to the musings of a man in love."

Nathan watched his friend slowly make his way across the great hall.

Declan, who had been conversing with Murray, shifted in his seat and called across the empty seats, "Already Caleb has had his share of other people's company, I see."

Nathan nodded, then turned and watched his friend step out into the courtyard. "Poor sod," he muttered, for he knew Caleb was about to learn that his problem couldn't be resolved by a flagon of wine and a hard sleep. Turning back to face Clan Brodie's captain, he asked, "Do ye think Lady Elora will grace us with her presence?"

"I have no memory of her missing the evening meal, not since she was a child anyway. But today has been particularly trying." Declan lifted his shoulders. "We will have to wait and see."

Then Murray added, "A missive arrived earlier today during the commotion. It was from Laird Mackintosh. Before supper I did meet with her about the matter, but she wasn't concerned. She said Egan had inquired about his so-called wedding present." Murray chuckled. "I promised to report how well the new mare had been received, and how much we are looking forward to the wealth of foals she will no doubt provide

Clan Brodie."

Declan nodded his approval. "It will serve him right to know how we have, as ye said, Nathan, taken his insult and made it our gain."

"Indeed," Nathan replied.

He fell into easy conversation with Declan and Murray while he waited, hoping that Elora would glide out from behind the screen and claim her seat next to his. But as the trestle tables began to empty and the villagers returned to their homes, it became clear that she was not going to make an appearance.

Incapable of waiting any longer, he made his excuses to the other men and hastened toward her chamber. Just as he was about to rap his knuckles on her door, it opened, but it was Mary who stepped out.

"Good eventide, Nathan." A basket of folded laundry was perched on her hip, but she still managed to curtsy.

"Good eventide, Mary."

Easing the door shut behind her, she said, "My lady is not in her chamber."

Brows drawn, he asked, "Do ye know if she is sitting with her sister?"

Mary shook her head. "Nay, I've just come from Lady Tempest's chamber and she was alone."

Nathan raked his hand through his hair. "Of course. Thank ye, Mary."

Mary curtsied again, then started down the hallway with her basket. But a moment later, she turned back around. "Often my lady will walk the battlements when she wishes to clear her head."

He dipped his head in thanks to Elora's young maid, then with renewed purpose, he continued his search. Taking the steps two at a time, he rounded the circular stairwell to the battlements. Several Brodie guards were in position, but Elora was nowhere to be seen. Next, he checked the solar and then the kitchen. When he still could not find her, he headed out into the courtyard where the guards at the front gate assured him that she had not left the castle.

He stiffened with frustration when, at last, he had to concede to the possibility that she was intentionally staying away from him. Standing in the great hall, his gaze was drawn to the door that led to the kitchen. His body ached with desire. His pulse raced. One visit to the buttery for a drink would take it all away. But he shook his head and took a deep breath. This time, he did not want his feelings to diminish.

Before he could change his mind, he turned on his heel and retreated up the stairs. After storming down the hallway, he threw open his chamber door and his breath hitched.

Lady Elora stood near the hearth, dressed in her linen night gown.

"Elora," he gasped.

She turned and their eyes locked. Without a word, she closed the distance between them and pressed herself against him. Rising up on her toes, bringing her lips a breath from his, she whispered, "Ye set my soul on fire."

A groan of ecstasy fled his lips as he crushed her against himself. His mouth descended on hers. He kissed her with all his hunger, all his need. Soft moans rose up from her throat as she met his passion with a fire all her own. Tearing their lips apart, she whispered, "I want to feel ye, skin to skin."

With a growl, he tore off his plaid and lifted her into his arms. He crossed the room and gently eased her down onto the bed. Then he kissed her with wild abandon. Her tongue met his, hungry and consuming. Her fingers wove through his hair, pressing herself harder against his body. He cupped her firm breast and she moaned, arching into his touch. His lips covered her nipple, flicking the hard peak through the fabric of her nightgown with his tongue. Her body pressed into his touch. "Closer," she begged.

A devilish smile curved his lips as he tore the fabric of her nightgown asunder. His mouth descended upon the rosy peak of her swollen nipple. His tongue caressing, suckling, teasing. Her soft moans of desire fueled his own hunger. His mouth devoured her, moving from one creamy mound to the other while his hands explored the soft lines of her waist and hips and the silken skin of her stomach.

She squirmed beneath him as she explored his body, her hands stroking the length of his back and curving over his bare shoulders. Fire spread where she touched, consuming, igniting his passion to greater heights. He burned with a need he had never known before. Passion raged through him. He had to touch and taste every inch of her.

~ * ~

Elora threw her head back as his lips explored her body, sending jolts of pleasure coursing through her. Then his touch journeyed over her stomach. His hands gripped her hips, which bucked of their own accord as the ache between her thighs became too much to bear. His tongue moved lower and lower until he parted her thighs. He nibbled at the sensitive skin of her inner thigh. She gripped the headboard, wild with desire. He was so close to where the ache surged with indescribable pain and pleasure. Then suddenly his mouth descended, and he tasted the very heat of her.

She cried out as sweet agony consumed her. He slowly stroked her sensitive womanhood with his tongue, delving deeper, teasing, tasting. Just when she thought the torment was too much, he shifted over her. She spread her legs wide as he guided his body into hers. His thick length burned, pressing deeper, stretching, hurting. She gripped his shoulders and held on tight. And then he burst through her innocence. She cried out. He froze, his body taut beneath her fingers. But after a few moments, the pain subsided and slowly, he began to move within her, thrusting, gently at first, then harder and harder. She gasped in sweet agony. Together, they moved, hot and hungry, soaring higher and higher as waves of ecstasy pulsed through her. And then she shattered, exploding with pleasure as his own cry of release mingled with hers in savage harmony.

# Chapter Seventeen

Elora awoke tucked snugly in the fold of Nathan's embrace. His body curved around hers from behind. She savored his closeness and the warmth of his steady breaths on the back of her neck. Closing her eyes, she inhaled his masculine scent. Her mind burned with the memory of his strong hands gently massaging her breasts, his tongue tasting and teasing as he journeyed down her neck to the rosy peaks of her nipples, then down to the curve of her hips and lower still. Just the memory made her body ache with desire. She remembered how he had let his plaid fall to the ground, revealing the sinewy lines and hard ridges of his muscular physique. The fire that he had ignited had built until she could no longer control herself.

More than anything, she wanted him to possess her again, to cry out her name as he had the night before.

But a new day was nearly upon them, bringing with it heartbreaking clarity.

She knew what she had to do.

A sharp pain cut through her heart as her thoughts turned to the inevitable. Choking back her tears, she slowly eased herself free from his arms and slid out of bed. Her footfalls were silent as she padded across the floor. At the door, she stopped and looked back at him. His black curls partially hid the sleek lines of his exquisite profile. The blanket slashed low on his hips, revealing his warrior's physique.

Her chest tightened, and a knot gathered in her throat. "I love ye," she whispered.

Then she straightened her back, steeled her shoulders, and opened the door. Forcing herself not to look back again, she eased the door closed and made her way to her chamber all the while feeling as if her heart was shattering into a million pieces.

Once in her room, she set to work, fearing that she might unravel if she paused for even a moment. Using water left over from her evening ablutions, she washed away the slickness between her thighs. Then, she crossed to her wardrobe and selected a deep blue tunic, over which she pulled on a surcote that laced on the sides. Using her fingers to untangle her curls, she wove her hair into a simple plait down her back. Swallowing hard, she opened the shutters and glanced out her casement. The hour was long before *Lauds*. With a deep breath, she turned away from the dark sky, opened her chamber door, and quietly made her way down to the solar.

Her heart pounded when she saw her table, for she knew what awaited her—a missive from Egan. Although she had told Murray that the chieftain of Clan Mackintosh had sent a smug message asking after the high-strung mare he had gifted their clan, that had been a lie. Sitting down at the table, her hand trembled as she picked up the parchment which spoke of the coming doom.

Through fresh tears, she read the blackguard's message again...

*Expect my coming the morrow following Easter when the Lenten season has passed.*

A weight settled in the pit of her stomach. The meaning of his words was clear. On that day she would be married—if not to someone else, then to him.

With a deep breath to quiet the torrent of emotion fighting to reach the surface of her heart and mind, she straightened her spine, steeled her shoulders, and reached for a clean piece of parchment. With her stony composure in place, she willed herself to make the sacrifice she knew she must. Dipping her quill in ink, she began to compose a new missive, one she believed would secure the best outcome for her people.

When she finished, she set her quill down and read over her words. For a moment, a breath, her selfish heart fought to be heard. Her chin quivered, but she clenched her jaw, fighting for calm.

She had to be strong for her people. She tilted her chin higher, assuring herself that in time, she would forget. But a sob pushed past her defenses. Her breath hitched.

She could never forget.

Dropping the missive on the table, she hung her head in her hands.

"Elora, what is it?"

With a startled gasp, Elora looked up and met her sister's gaze. Tempest hastened across the room.

Elora took a deep breath. "Ye should be in bed."

Tempest waved away her concern. "I slept most of yesterday and all through the night." Then she squeezed Elora's hands. "What is it? Tell me what weighs on ye so."

Elora shook her head stiffly, struggling to contain her emotions.

"Ye promised not to shut me out again," Tempest reminded

her. "We need each other."

Elora slumped back in her chair. "Ye're right," she said softly. She pressed her hand to her forehead. "Ye know why I have a distaste for marriage, but I've never told ye this." She took a deep breath. "Before she died, mum made me promise her that I would never marry."

Tempest expelled a long breath. "But, Elora, 'tis an impossible promise for a lady to keep."

Elora straightened in her seat and looked her sister dead on. "I have labored and labored for a way to keep my promise—not only to honor our mother's final wishes—but to safeguard our people. Imagine what could befall our clan should I surrender my will and judgment to the wrong man." Elora stood and began pacing the room. "Make no mistake, once I vow to honor and obey my husband, I lose all control." She whirled around and met her sister's wide gaze. "And if I choose poorly, then what? Do I go back to the days of slinking behind a tyrant's back to ensure my people arc clothed and fed?"

Tempest scrunched her brow. "I understand yer fears, Elora, but I do not see how we can carry on for much longer without a laird. Egan has made his intentions clear. And when word spreads of our vulnerability, other chieftains will set their sights on our lands."

"Ye're right," Elora said softly. She sat down again. "I have no choice but to break my promise." She handed Egan's missive to her sister who quickly opened it and scanned the page.

"That scoundrel," Tempest snapped as she stood and started to pace the room while she read. Then her eyes flashed wide. "He writes to say that he journeys here the day after Easter."

She nodded. "My time is up. It would seem as I have no choice but to marry William Grant."

Tempest whirled around. "What?"

Elora gave her sister a challenging look. "I have to make the choice that is right for our people. It will be years before William comes of age—years that I can lead our clan without hindrance. And by the time he is old enough to take on the role of laird, I will have had time to train him properly."

Tempest shook her head. "But ye love Nathan. Ye cannot deny yer feelings to me!"

"My feelings are unimportant," Elora snapped. "They come second to the wellbeing of the clan."

Tempest's eyes flashed with passion. "How can ye say that? Ye speak as though ye're somehow separate when ye're as much a part of this clan as any other man, woman, or child."

Elora shook her head. "Ye don't understand."

"Don't say that," Tempest hissed, slamming her hand on the table. "Yer fear is lying to ye, making ye believe ye have no choice." Tempest's eyes became beseeching. She circled around the table and knelt at her sister's feet. "Hear my words, Elora," she began softly. "Yer heart is good and true. Ye want everything for me and for our clan, but nothing for yerself." Tempest seized her sister's hands. "Let yerself matter, and ye will be a better lady for it."

Elora swallowed hard. "I...I don't know how?"

Tempest cupped her cheek. "Start by listening to yer own heart. Ye love Nathan."

Tears stung Elora's eyes. "But what do I really know of him? Other than he's a renegade who left his clan. For pity's sake, I found him in a tavern, draped by whores and drowning in his cups. How can I be sure he will be a fair leader?"

"Aren't we all drowning in something?" Tempest asked pointedly. "For years, ye've been suffocated by yer own rigidity whilst I've been struggling beneath the weight of self-pity. Whatever Nathan has been running from, ye cannot deny that he is a good man with a kind heart. What more could we hope for in a laird?"

Elora closed her eyes, returning in her mind to a place where Nathan's strong arms surrounded her, where his kiss made her wild with need, and where his body set hers free.

Could she really choose love?

She eyed the two missives on the table, afraid that somehow the oppression the letters represented could somehow reach out beyond the page and snatch her free will.

"Elora, look at me," Tempest said firmly, drawing Elora's gaze. "Trust more, fear less."

Her sister's beautiful face blurred as a fresh wave of tears flooded Elora's eyes. "How did ye grow to be such an amazing woman?"

Tempest smiled. "I've had the most selfless, strong, and determined older sister to emulate." Her smile stretched wider. "Do ye trust me?"

Elora blinked away her tears, took a deep breath, and smiled. "Aye, I trust ye."

Tempest's face brightened even more. "Come on," she said, laughing as she seized Elora's hand and pulled her toward the door. "I know just what ye need at this moment."

Never letting go of her hand, Tempest led Elora through the sleepy castle to the stables. Together, they saddled Rosie and Hazel, but before they mounted their mares, Tempest rushed to Storm's stall. "Do not fash yerself, lass. Once my head is fully healed, I'll ride ye clear to the Firth of Moray."

Elora called to her sister. "I'm ready."

Tempest turned and passed a scrutinizing gaze over Elora.

"Not quite."

Her sister's nimble fingers made quick work of the laces on Elora's surcote, which was soon cast over the side of a stall. Then, she loosened Elora's braid, letting her hair fall unbound down her back.

Tempest smiled. "Now, ye're ready."

Once they passed through the gates and circled around the outer wall, they set out at a trot. Darkness still blanketed the land, painting the earth in shades of silver and violet. Stars shone brightly overhead, and yet the sky at the horizon had begun to lighten, revealing dawn's promise. Elora breathed deep this promise—a new dawn meant a new day and a new life, in which fear would no longer be her guide.

When they reached the last field, rolling moorland stretched out before them. Tempest reined her horse in. Fire lit her blue eyes. "I dare not gallop until my wound has fully healed. But ye, Elora, ye must! Go! Ride! Lose yerself! Only then will ye find yer joy!"

The wind picked up, lifting Elora's unbound hair. A shiver coursed up her spine as she held her sister's powerful gaze.

"I love ye, Tempest," she said, her heart full. Then she shifted her gaze to the distant moors where a streak of fiery light now ignited the horizon. Adjusting the grip on her reins, laughter bubbled up her throat. Then she threw her head back and whooped to the sky and drove her heels into Rosie's flanks, setting out across the sea of dusky hills. A thrill shot through her. The wind whipped her hair. For the first time in her life, she felt free and fluid as a wave crashing toward shore. Her passion unleashed, she cried out, "Faster, Rosie!"

Cresting to the top of a grassy swell, she reined in her mount and gazed at the beauty of their land, Clan Brodie's land. Tears streamed down her face, but they were not tears of suffering as her mother's tears had always been.

They were tears of triumph.

Tears of joy.

She threw her arms wide. Her joy was inside herself, and all she had to do was let it come to the surface. She could feel the walls of her constraint crumble. No longer would she rely on control and rigidity to protect herself. She was part of a clan. Just as she had always cared for her people and raised them high, she, too, could count on her kinfolk in times of need.

And then silver eyes, raw and honest, came to the fore of her thoughts. "And I have love," she whispered aloud.

Without hesitation, she turned Rosie around and raced back the way she'd come. Reining in her mount beside Tempest, she burst out, "I found my joy!"

"In the ride?" Tempest asked.

Elora shook her head. "Nay, I found it in me."

Her sister's smile widened.

"Come on, Tempest. There is a man awaiting me at Castle Bròn who I plan to marry, but not days from now when the Lenten season ends. I'm going to ask him to marry me this very day."

Her face beaming, Tempest looked Elora dead on. "Now who's the renegade?"

# Chapter Eighteen

Nathan stirred from sleep and reached out, searching the bed for silken skin and gentle curves, but when his hand grazed naught but cold linen, his eyes flew open. Jerking upright, he scanned the room.

Worry furrowed his brow. What had happened? Why had she left?

But then his shoulders eased as he remembered that each day at Castle Bròn began in the same way. When the chapel bell sounded the hour for *Prime*, Abagail, a young serving lass with hair the color of straw and a smattering of freckles across her nose, always rapped on his door. More often than not, her gentle knock roused him from sleep. He would then sit up in bed and make certain the blanket was pulled to his waist before he called for her to enter. Without fail, the moment her wee face peeked into the room and met his gaze, a blush crept across her cheeks. Then she would look away and dart into the room like a wee mouse to set a pitcher of fresh water on the table near the hearth. And with a quick curtsy, she would take her leave, never once meeting his gaze again.

Nathan chuckled aloud as an image entered his mind of Abagail peeking into the room to find him and Elora in bed together, naked, their limbs entwined. No doubt, Elora had pictured that very thing when she had awoken and made her way back to her chamber. After all, they were not supposed to be officially wed until after Easter.

He lay back and counted the days until he could officially call Elora his wife. It was Maundy Thursday, the first day of the Triduum, which marked the start of the three days leading up to Easter. The morrow would bring Good Friday and then Holy Saturday, which meant in four days' time, he and Elora would be husband and wife.

His smile could not be contained as he swung his legs over the side of the bed. Closing his eyes, he savored his memories of the night before. The feel of her soft thighs wrapped around his waist. Her lids were half closed over blue eyes that burned with savage fire, beckoning and hungry. Her soft moans and the feel of her nails raking down his back. He could still feel her curves melting to his form as they fell asleep together, replete from their shared pleasure.

His heart racing, he fell back on the bed, wishing she were still there so that he could make her cry out again and again. "And again," he whispered.

Eager to see her, he jerked upright and reached for his plaid. It was then he noticed the fabric on the floor. The soft linen with lace trim could only be a piece of Elora's nightgown, which he had torn to reveal her glorious nakedness. Picking the fabric off the ground, he quickly located the other piece, which was still on the bed. He seized it so that he might hide the evidence of their lovemaking, but when he lifted it away from the mattress, he revealed a much bigger testament of the consummation of their marriage—the stain of her maidenhead on his sheet.

He faltered, then tapped his fingers on his chin as he decided his next move. With only one clear solution in sight, he stripped the sheet from the bed and bundled it together with the torn nightgown. His gaze darted around the room as he searched for a hiding place. Crossing to the chest where he had stored his few belongings, he removed his cloak, sporran, and saddlebags and placed the evidence of their lovemaking inside. Then he covered the bundle with his effects so that no one would know what had occurred the night before.

Closing the lid, he chuckled to himself as he pictured them pulling the stained sheet out of the chest on their official wedding night and spreading it over the mattress for the servants to find the following morning. Eager to share his humorous plan with his bride, he left his chamber behind to go in search of Elora.

He whistled as he hastened down the hallway, greeting those he passed with a smile. With so many servants bustling through the halls, he knew it must be after *Lauds* but still before *Prime* because Abagail had yet to knock on his door, and so he headed straight to the solar where Elora was likely having her morning meeting with Murray. Finding the door closed, he rapped on the slatted wood and waited for permission to enter.

"Please, come in," called a voice laced with desperation.

He flung the door wide. Smoke came billowing out into the hallway. Seizing the upper folds of his plaid to cover his face. He hastened into the room, crossed to the casement, and threw open the shutters. Then he whirled around. The room was empty but for Mary who was retreating away from the smoking hearth, coughing and sputtering.

"Mary," he called and reached for her hand, drawing her close to the window. Turning, he yanked a tapestry down from the wall and used it to smother the smoking embers in the hearth.

As the air began to clear, he helped Mary over to one of the high-backed chairs.

"Thank ye," she gasped. "The flue…it must need cleaning."

Nathan squatted down in front of her. "Shall I send for the midwife?"

"Nay," Mary coughed. "Ye needn't bother. I will ask Agnes to brew me a tisane."

He squeezed her hand encouragingly, then stood. "I will speak to Agnes on yer behalf, and I'll fetch Elora. No doubt, she'll want to see for herself that ye're all right."

Mary shook her head. "She and Tempest are out riding. Ye needn't trouble yerself. I will just rest here a while."

"'Tis no trouble, Mary," He reassured her and crossed to Elora's table where he took up a pitcher of water. As he started to pour the young maid a cup, his thoughts drifted to why the sisters had set out for a ride so early in the day. But then he drew a sharp breath. Wind sliced through the room from the open casement, scattering Elora's missives and lists to the floor.

"Oh dear," Mary exclaimed, jumping to her feet.

"Nay, Mary," he said firmly. "Sit. I will tidy yer lady's desk."

As he stacked the larger pieces of parchment together, his gaze passed over the scrawled message on top, and he realized it was the missive from Laird Mackintosh that Murray had remarked upon at supper the evening before, except there was no mention of the chestnut mare. Nathan's gaze narrowed on the laird's thinly veiled threat.

"The blackguard," he growled and set the stack on the table, placing the heavy clay pitcher on top of the pages to keep them from flying away again. While he started to turn a plan to deal with Egan over in his mind, he continued to gather the other pages, many of them smaller pieces. He shook his head lovingly at Elora's precise handwriting.

He smiled at Mary. "She does enjoy her lists."

Mary chuckled. "Aye, that she does."

"I wonder what she will plan for today…" His words trailed off as he skimmed another page.

His stomach dropped out.

"Does she play me for a fool?" he snarled, whirling around to face Mary.

Her eyes flashed wide. "Whatever do ye mean?"

He shoved the missive in front of her face. "Yer lady intends to marry another."

Mary shook her head vehemently. "She intends nothing of the sort."

"Look at the date," he snapped. "She composed this letter this very morning."

Mary inhaled sharply. "But…there must be some kind of mistake." She stood and started to hasten across the room. "Let us go and find her. I'm certain she'll be able to explain."

He crumpled the page in his fist. "Her intentions are clear."

Turning on his heel, the wadded parchment dropped from his fingers as he stormed back to his chamber. Throwing open the chest, he seized his effects, uncovering the stained sheet and torn nightgown. Her words from the night before came unbidden to his mind.

*Ye set my soul on fire.*

Apparently, the fire had already been snuffed out, because she must have left his bed and gone straight to the solar to compose her letter accepting marriage to another man.

"Lies," he growled as he secured his sporran around his waist. Then he slung his cloak and saddlebags over his shoulder and marched back the way he'd come. Barreling through the castle halls, he ignored the greetings of those he passed. Blood pounded in his ears as he thundered down the steps to the courtyard.

"Good morrow, Nathan," Declan called.

Without a word, Nathan brushed past the older man and headed straight for the stables.

"Caleb," he bellowed.

"Aye," his friend called from one of the stalls where he was brushing his horse's coat.

Nathan stormed toward him. "Get yer things! We're leaving!"

Caleb's eyes flashed wide. "What happened?"

"I'm in no mood for questions," Nathan snarled, throwing open the stall door to ready his own mount. His hands shook with rage as he saddled his horse. After securing his saddlebags, he swung up in place and met Caleb's dazed gaze. "Meet me at Fenhorn. Do not delay." Then he drove his heels into his horse's flanks. Keeping low in his saddle, he charged out into the courtyard and straight through the front gates, ignoring the alarmed cries of the Brodie villagers and warriors as he raced past.

~ * ~

Nathan rode hard through Brodie lands, heading northeast to the hamlet of Fenhorn. The small settlement was on Sutherland lands, but its few inhabitants hailed from several different clans close to the region, that of Sutherland, Dunbar, Innes, and Cumming. The one tavern in the hamlet, The Siren's Song, was owned by Samuel Cumming, and it was where Nathan and his band of thief-takers had met with Laird Cumming to discuss the Bowie contract. Nathan remembered that Samuel poured a full tankard, his serving lasses were fine to look upon, and the room where he had stayed had been free of fleas. There could be no better place to hold up and empty his heart and mind of all traces of her.

Bending low in his saddle, he pushed his horse harder across the moors as he strained to outrun the memory of her touch, her tender whispers, and the moments of pure joy that had filled his heart. Growling, he drove his heels into his horse's flanks, cursing his foolishness for ever believing Lady Elora Brodie could love a man like him.

~ * ~

When he at last reached Fenhorn, the sun was high in the sky and his horse labored to breathe. At the livery, he gave the stable master a pouch of silver to ensure the best care for his mount.

"I'm sorry, my friend," he whispered softly, pressing his forehead to his horse's muzzle. Then he left and made his way to The Siren's Song.

The tavern was busy with patrons seeking their afternoon meal. He crossed the room to the bar. "I remember ye," Samuel said when he spied Nathan's approach. "Ye're the thief-taker."

Nathan nodded.

"Aye, I remember ye were generous with yer coin and gentle with my lassies." Samuel set a tankard of ale in front of Nathan. "Consider this first one a gift."

Without reply, Nathan set a few pennies on the bar, despite Samuel's generosity, then turned to find a table. Straightaway, two lassies flanked him, each taking an arm. He let them lead him like something adrift on the waves to a table in the back. Easing into a chair, he rested his head on the wall behind him and closed his eyes.

The women crooned promises of pleasure in his ears while they caressed his shoulders and pressed feather soft kisses to his neck. But despite their tender administrations, their words barely penetrated his mind, nor could he truly feel their touch. The empty pit in his stomach expanded, wider and wider, stretching to his heart, until there was nothing.

He gripped the handle of his tankard. "All is as it should be," he muttered bitterly.

Slowly, he lifted the tankard to his lips. But then the door swung wide, and Caleb walked into the tavern. When they locked eyes, his friend barreled across the room. "What in the blazes are ye doing here?"

"Sit down," Nathan drawled, using his foot to push out the chair across from him.

"Are ye a fool?" Caleb exclaimed.

Nathan narrowed his eyes on Caleb. "Do I look satisfied?"

His blue eyes ablaze with feeling, Caleb, quickly sat and looked Nathan hard in the eye. "Before I left the stables, Declan and Mary found me, and Mary told me about the letter."

Nathan shook his head, a mirthless laugh fleeing his lips as he raised his cup to take a sip. "So, now ye know. Do ye intend to gloat and tell me I was a fool to ever accept the job?"

Caleb shook his head. "I do not understand ye. How could ye just leave like that?"

Nathan leaned forward in his seat. "She lied to me," he hissed. "She's never been opposed to marriage. She just never wanted to marry me, a worthless thief-taker."

Caleb's eyes flashed wide. "How can ye say that?"

Nathan narrowed his eyes on his friend. "Because she has accepted another man's offer of marriage."

"Ahh…" Caleb said leaning back in his seat, his expression softening. "Now I understand."

"What?" Nathan snapped.

"Ye don't know."

Nathan slammed his fist on the table. "Ye push too far, Caleb! Say whatever is on yer mind and be done with it!"

"William Grant is not a man. He's a child."

Nathan faltered. "What do ye mean he's a child?"

"He is naught but ten and three," Caleb said softly.

The pit of Nathan's stomach dropped out. "But…but Clan Grant is half the size of Egan's. 'Tis madness."

Caleb shook his head. "Nay, not madness. She's afraid, Nathan. Naught but fear made this choice, nothing more."

Nathan raked his hand through his hair. "Egan is certain to take offense."

Caleb nodded. "He'll be furious, and her only protection will be the name of a child."

His heart pounding in his ears, Nathan stood, shrugging off the now cloying hands of the serving wenches. Head low, eyes straight on, he stormed out of The Siren's Song without a backward glance.

"We'll need fresh horses," he barked as Caleb joined him outside.

"Already done," Caleb said, crossing to a nearby hitching post where two, sinewy stallions were tethered.

Nathan swung up in the saddle. His nostrils flared as he met Caleb's gaze. "If Egan, or anyone else, harms her, I will slice them into pieces and scatter their remains for buzzards to feast upon."

A glint of humor lit Caleb's gaze. "So, what yer saying is that ye're in love with Elora?"

"Completely," Nathan replied. Then, he drove his heels into his horse's flanks and raced back over the very hills he had only just traversed.

# Chapter Nineteen

Elora and Tempest thundered through the gates of Castle Bròn. Sliding down from Rosie's back, Elora handed the reins off to Jacob. "We'll both need fresh mounts," she insisted.

"Aye, my lady," Jacob answered quickly before hastening toward the stables with their tired mares in tow.

"We should see if Declan has returned," Tempest said breathlessly, drawing Elora's gaze.

Elora nodded, but then movement caught her eye and she turned to see Mary rushing down the castle steps. "My ladies, I'm so glad ye're both back. Supper is waiting for ye in the great hall."

Elora shook her head. "We haven't time."

Mary seized Elora's hand. "Please, my lady. Ye've been racing over the moors with naught to eat but a crumb of bannock. The sun is beginning its descent. Come and rest a while. Let the men search for Nathan."

Elora looked to the west. The sun was indeed beginning to dip in the sky. Her chest tightened, and her mind returned to earlier in the day, when she and Tempest had first raced back home after their exhilarating morning ride. Elora had thundered through the gate and planned to march straight into the castle, throw her arms around Nathan's neck, and ask him to take her to the chapel that very moment.

But Declan had been awaiting her return.

When she had slid down from Rosie's back, he drew close. She had known something terrible had happened the moment she met his fretful gaze. And then he spoke the words that had stolen her breath and bent her over with searing pain as if he had plunged a dagger straight through her beating heart...*Nathan is gone.*

Elora shook her head, forcing her thoughts back to the present. She turned to Mary. "It was my own weakness that drove him from my side," Elora insisted. "I am to blame. I lost faith in him, in myself—"

"And now ye must have faith in yer men." Mary interjected. "Declan is out there with a dozen warriors. They will find Nathan." Then she bowed her head and dipped in a quick curtsy. "Forgive me for interrupting and for telling ye what ye should do, my lady."

Elora took a deep breath, and then reached for Mary, pulling her maid into a warm embrace. "I'm realizing more and more that at times I must stop and heed someone else's advice." Elora drew back slightly and smiled gently. "Thank ye." Expelling a slow breath, she turned to Tempest. "Shall we rest and eat?"

Elora could see Tempest hesitate. She took in her sister's worried brow. "Declan will find them," Elora said reassuringly, and then for Tempest's ears alone, she whispered, "He will bring Caleb back."

Tempest held her sister's gaze, and Elora was struck by the depth of feeling she glimpsed in her sister's eyes. "Ye've grown so much, so strong and beautiful. Ye're not a child anymore."

155

Elora squeezed Tempest's hand. "Hold tight to yer faith and I'll hold tight to mine. All right?"

Taking a deep breath, Tempest nodded, and the worry in her expression eased. "I know Declan will find them," she said bravely as she clasped Elora's hand and started to lead her toward the castle steps.

But Elora held back and shook her head. "Ye go ahead. I will be in directly."

Elora watched as Tempest and Mary climbed the steps together and disappeared into the great hall. Her stomach growled with hunger, but before she retired to the keep, she had one more thing to do.

Turning on her heel, she crossed the courtyard and entered the chapel. Her footfalls echoed off the high ceiling as she made her way to the side altar and lit a fresh candle from one that was nearly burned down to its wick. Then she sat down and let the quiet of the chapel surround her as she tried to calm her racing heart.

It was Maundy Thursday, which meant that in four days' time, Laird Mackintosh would arrive at Castle Bròn. Her heart and body belonged to Nathan. She could not marry Egan, but she also could not prove that Nathan and she were officially wed, not unless she retrieved the stained sheet that she had discovered in Nathan's room when she had first gone there to find him.

"What a fool I've been," she muttered. Despite how she tried to hold tight to her faith, it took all her strength not to despair. What if she had lost him forever?

Her breath hitched as the door swung wide and thunderous footfalls suddenly echoed around her. Fearing that Egan had come early, her heart raced as she whirled around.

She gasped. It was Declan. He was breathless, and a frown shaped his countenance. She slumped in her seat and watched the warriors file into the chapel. Declan held her gaze. She could tell he wished to speak to her, but he held back—doubtless because he did not want to tell her that his search had been fruitless. Declan turned away suddenly. Her gaze followed his to the shadowy outline of a man with broad shoulders filling the arched doorway. The man stepped inside, revealing black curls and silver eyes, which narrowed on her. She inhaled sharply as Nathan thundered into the room.

Her heart leapt at the sight of him. She wanted to run into his embrace, but the fury on his face made her falter. Her chest tightened. Now, she knew why Declan's expression had appeared so grim. Clearly, this was not the happy reunion of her dreams.

Wringing her hands, she started toward him, "Nathan—" she began, her eyes wide.

But he thrust his hand out. "Nay," he growled. "I am going to speak and ye're going to listen."

His breaths came in great heaves. He closed the distance between them. Her hands ached to reach out and touch him, but his gaze bore into hers with a hardness that stole her breath. "Elora," he began, but then he expelled a slow breath. At length, his expression softened. He reached for her hand. "Ye don't have to marry Egan or William Grant, and ye don't have to marry me."

Her breath caught. She shook her head. "But—"

Again, he held up his hand to silence her. "Hear me out."

He dropped to one knee. "I swear my fealty to Clan Brodie and to ye," he vowed. Then he withdrew the sword strapped to his back and laid it at her feet. "I pledge to ye my sword. With

157

my life or my death, I will defend yer keep, yer people, and yer freedom."

Her heart swelled. Tears stung her eyes, and she let them fall without constraint. She was done holding back, especially where Nathan was concerned.

Dropping to her knees, she threw her arms around his neck and pressed her lips to his. He stiffened in her arms, but only for a moment. Then, he crushed her against his hard chest, deepening their kiss. An instant later, he tore his lips free. Brows drawn, he cupped her cheeks. "I…I do not understand."

Her tears renewed. "When Declan told me that ye left, I thought…I thought I would surely die. I couldn't see how I could go on, knowing that ye were out there somewhere, not loving me back."

His eyes brightened. "Elora!" He seized her again, pressing her against him and kissed her lips with velvety softness. Then he pulled a breath away. His gaze sought hers. "I thought ye couldn't love a man like me."

Her fingers gripped his tunic. "Ye're a good, kind man, Nathan, and I love ye. I love ye with all that I am and all I hope to be."

Forehead to forehead, she watched as a smile broke across his face and lit his eyes with a joy that made her feel as if she was still at risk of dying, but not from heartache. Surely, she would be crushed beneath the might of her love. "I'm going to burst into a million stars right here in yer arms."

His eyes burned into her soul. "Ye're as beautiful as starlight and as warm as the summer sun," he whispered. "I don't deserve ye." His brows drew together, and pain flashed in his gaze. "But will ye have me, thief-taker and all?"

She wrapped her arms around his neck seductively. "I already have," she whispered in his ear. "And there's a sheet hidden away in a chest in yer room that proves it."

His face grew serious and for her ears alone, he said, "I will not force my claim because of the night we shared together. I want our marriage to be of yer choosing."

She cupped his cheeks between her hands. "I choose ye, Nathan Campbell." Then she backed out of his embrace and set her hands on her hips. "Right away, in fact."

She turned to Declan. "Please go find the priest." Then she addressed the band of Brodie warriors standing in the nave. "Go, all of ye, and spread the word. Nathan and I are to be wed this day, this very moment, in fact."

Nathan held out a calming hand. "We can wait. I'm sure ye had a special tunic in mind and a menu and—"

"And none of that matters." She met his gaze straight on. "Nathan, before the sun had fully risen, I vowed I would marry ye this very day." She crossed her arms over her chest. "So, what say ye? Will ye have me?"

He seized her, sweeping her off her feet. "Aye, Elora Brodie, with all my heart."

~ * ~

Reeking of horses and sweat and clad in naught but a dirty tunic, Elora stood with Declan in preparation of walking through the chapel nave, which was filled with her kin, to take her place with Nathan at the altar.

"Hold still," Declan said, chuckling as he plucked a burr from her tangled, unbound curls. His eyes crinkled as he smiled at her. "I never imagined walking ye down the aisle like this," he said, glancing down at his own soiled clothing.

159

Laughter bubbled up her throat. "We are a mess, to be sure."

The older man shook his head. "Nay, my lady. I meant only me." Tears flooded his eyes as he grazed his rugged hand down her cheek. "Wearing that bright smile, Ye've never looked lovelier."

She reached out and clasped the older man's hands. "Thank ye, Declan." Her voice dropped to a whisper. "Thank ye for always believing in me."

He smiled warmly. "Even when ye were just a wee lass, ye put everyone else's happiness first." He offered her his arm. "'Tis yer turn, my lady."

Her bottom lip quivered as she wove her arm through his. "I love ye, Declan."

His eyes widened. "I love ye, my lady, but I didn't mean to make ye cry, too."

She laughed through her tears. "My eyes have been dry for far too long. From now on, ye'll see my tears and hear my laughter, and after that gorgeous man standing down there is officially my husband, ye're going to see me dance!"

Declan threw his head back with laughter. "That I must see." He patted her hand tenderly. "Shall we?"

She swallowed hard and nodded. Her stomach fluttered as they started down the aisle. She locked eyes with Nathan, and when, at last, she faced him, she threw her arms around his neck and kissed him with all her love, all her passion.

"Ahem." Father Paul cleared his throat. Laughter emanated from where the villagers stood.

Nathan gently tugged his lips free. "I think the kiss is supposed to come after we make our vows."

A slow smile curved her lips as she continued to keep her arms around his neck. "We've both broken our fair share of rules."

His smile shone in his silver eyes. "What's one more," he added with a shrug and crushed her against his hard chest, bent her back, and kissed her until her toes curled. The villagers erupted in cheers.

Their chests heaving, Nathan pulled her upright. Then, together, they faced the priest.

Father Paul raised a stern brow at them both, but he could not hide the smile that tugged at his lips. "Are ye certain, ye wish to wed this night?"

"Aye," both Elora and Nathan answered in unison.

"We'll be good, Father. I promise," Elora said, doing her best to bring a touch of decorum to her stance.

Her gaze held Nathan's while the ceremony commenced. It was all she could do not to kiss him again and again as she made her vows. And when Father Paul announced that they were at last husband and wife, and he bade Nathan kiss the bride, her breath caught.

Slowly, he lowered his lips to hers. With tender reverence, he kissed her, the touch a feather soft caress. Then, he drew away and rested his forehead on hers. "I can't believe it."

"What?" she whispered.

"That ye would choose me."

She placed his hand on her beating heart. "Do ye feel that?"

He nodded.

"Na—than." She patted his hand in rhythm to her own heart. "Na—than." And then a smile curved her lips. "My heart beats for ye."

Laughing, he scooped her into his arms and spun her around. "Now, can I take ye to my bed?"

"Ahem."

They both turned their heads and looked at the priest. "Sorry, Father," she said.

"Sorry, Father," he repeated and started to carry her back down the aisle.

"To answer yer question," she began and shifted her gaze to look at Tempest, "first we dance!"

~ * ~

There were no strings of garland decorating the great hall. The fare on the tables was simple. Still, the great hall of Castle Bròn had never been livelier or so full of joy, graced as it was by the lady of the keep kicking up her heels and circling in a reel with her kin. And when the hour grew late, and everyone had eaten their fill, the villagers bade the happy couple goodnight.

"Now is the hour when ye can sweep me into yer arms," Elora said, wrapping her arms around his neck.

"And carry ye to my bed," he said in a husky voice as he scooped her off the ground.

Their eyes locked. He carried her to his chamber and set her feet down in front of the hearth. Slowly, tenderly, they undressed each other, their gazes never parting. Then he swept his arm under her knees and lifted her, cradling her as he crossed the room to his bed and laid her gently down. "Ye're so beautiful," he rasped.

Her heart swelled. She threaded her fingers through his black curls and pressed her lips to his. The tip of his tongue ran playfully along the lines of her mouth like a whispered caress. She parted her lips. His tongue stroked hers. She moaned softly, wrapping her arms around his neck and pressing herself into him, surrendering to the passion of their kiss. Sensation spread throughout her whole body like a storm unleashed.

His strong hands raked over her waist and hips with possessive strength. The corded muscles along his back shifted beneath her fingers as she clung to him, stroking his hot skin. His hand curved around her breast, caressing, teasing. She gasped and arched her back into his touch, needing him, wanting him. Then his hand stroked over her stomach and grazed between her legs. Her breath caught. Their eyes locked. His silver gaze burned through her as he parted her legs. Her body ached for his. Breathless, she gripped his shoulders. "I need ye," she cried.

"I need ye," he echoed.

He stretched over her, his gaze boring into hers, wild and demanding. She opened her legs wider with wanton abandon. Positioning himself between her thighs, he entered her slowly, deliberately. She cried out with hunger, wanting him to fill her. The ache within her demanded the fullness of his hard length. She wrapped her legs around his waist. Fire, red-hot, raged throughout her body. She thrust her hips against him. "Please," she begged.

He thrust deep and hard. She cried out, clinging to him. He thrust deeper, harder. Her body ached. Her heart pounded. Her nails carved into his shoulders. Together, they soared, reaching, climbing, needing, until they cried out, raw and wild, and found their release in each other's arms.

When her breaths had evened out and her heart ceased to race, she curled into him, resting her head on his strong chest. She played with the crisp black hair over his beating heart.

"I love ye," he breathed.

Rolling onto her stomach. She rested her chin in her hand. "I love ye," she replied. Her face ached from smiling, but it was the sweetest pain she had ever known. "Ye make me so happy," she said.

He bit his bottom lip as his hungry gaze raked over her. "I intend to make ye happy again and again tonight."

She squealed and pushed him away playfully, but he seized her waist and pulled her beneath him.

"Just help me to remember one thing," he bade her.

"Anything," she promised.

A spark of mischief entered his eye. "We have to dig out that sheet from the chest and spread it over the bed to be found on the morrow."

Laughter burst from her lips. "Are ye protecting my reputation?"

"With my life or my death, I have vowed to protect ye," he said. Then his face grew serious. He stroked her cheek. "And I always will. Ye're not alone anymore, Elora."

"And neither are ye," she rasped. "Together, there is nothing we can't accomplish."

"Starting with…" His words trailed off as he began a new trail of kisses down her throat stirring the fiery passion that had always burned deep within her soul.

A passion only her renegade could ignite.

# Chapter Twenty

Good Friday and Holy Saturday were marked by Clan Brodie with great solemnity. Nathan found himself more reflective on those final days of the Triduum than he ever had been in the past. His heart was full of gratitude for his beautiful bride, and for the welcome he had received from her kinfolk. Still, the mournful services and quiet darkness of the chapel steered his thoughts away from the joy of the present, leading him back to days of regret. Once again, he found himself plagued by the lingering shadow of a heart-shaped face, black curls, and innocent blue eyes.

On the eve of Easter, following a day of fasting and reflection, he lay in bed with Elora. Gazing up at the ceiling with one arm at rest over his head, he held her close with his other arm while she rested her head on his chest.

"Who is Cait?" she asked suddenly.

He froze. His heart pounded in his ears. "How do ye know about Cait?"

She bent her neck back to look up at him. "Last night ye said her name in yer sleep."

Easing her off his chest, he sat up and swung his legs over the side of the bed and rested his head in his hands. Elora came up behind him and gently caressed his shoulders and arms. "Tell me," she bade him softly.

He closed his eyes against the pain. "I've never spoken of her."

She reached out and gently turned his chin so that he met her gaze, and with soft insistence, she whispered, "Tell me."

"Cait was my half-sister." His hands clenched into tight fists. Anger seethed inside his heart, anger at himself. He cleared his throat and blew out a long breath, trying to control the storm of emotion churning within his heart.

If he was going to tell Elora, he knew he needed to start at the beginning. Keeping his gaze downcast he said, "My mother died giving birth to me." He lifted his shoulders. "My father blamed me for her death."

She gasped. "Did he say as much?"

Nathan shook his head. "Not with words, but…" His heart raced as he struggled to go on. "Whenever he looked at me, which was a rare occurrence, hatred shone in his eyes." He took another deep breath before he continued. "As a child I knew his regard for me was different than the love and affection he showed my older brothers."

He paused for a moment, allowing his heart to be soothed by her hand gently stroking his back. "Eventually, he remarried. On my tenth birthday, his new wife bore him a daughter." His chest tightened. "They called her Cait." The ache in his heart became unbearable. Still, he pushed on. "She was joyful and spirited like Tempest. Everyone adored her, doted on her…even me." His nostrils flared. "But as I grew older, eventually my resentment toward my father consumed me. His hatred for me had taken root in my heart, and I became someone not deserving of love. I was defiant and reckless."

"Ye were a child," she interjected. "Every child deserves love."

"Aye," he said. "But I didn't remain a child. When I turned ten and six, I left to make my own fortune as a hired sword. For nearly eight years, I partnered with a man...Brogan MacDonell." The name came out as a snarl. For a moment, he could not speak as he fought for calm. Closing his eyes, he focused on steadying his racing heart. "Brogan was two years older than me. He was powerful and arrogant, and together, we earned a great fortune. Wanting to prove my worth to my father, I returned home and brought Brogan with me."

He hung his head in his hands. "He was a rake and a scoundrel, this much I knew. My brothers and father warned me of his character, but I only took their words as spite against me." A mirthless laugh fled his lips. "But none of us, not even I, knew how treacherous a man Brogan truly was."

Nathan stiffened. His stomach twisted. "Cait fell victim to his charms. In the dead of night, she ran away with him. We tracked them as far as Loch Linnhe where they had taken a ferry bound for the Isle of Islay." He swallowed hard. "But a storm overturned the boat." The sting of tears burned his eyes as he remembered. "Everyone on board drowned."

"Nay," Elora gasped.

"Cait was but ten and four."

Tears flooded her eyes as she reached for him, but he gently pushed her away. "Now, ye know." He sat straight and raked his hand through his hair.

She drew close and placed her hand on his heart. "Ye look at me, Nathan. Ye're not to blame for her death. The only one who should bear the weight of blame is Brogan himself, and he is already dead."

"Blame has been placed on my head, not only by me, but by my family. When we learned what happened, my father banished

167

me that very day. In his eyes, I killed her."

"But ye didn't!"

He expelled a long breath. "Ye're right. I did not kill her. But I did set in motion the events that led to her death."

Shaking her head, she opened her mouth as if to refute him, but he held up his hands to stay her words. "I know ye want to take that truth away from me, but ye can't, nor should ye." He took a deep breath and straightened. "I've been running from it for seven long years now. I must accept my part." He lifted his shoulders. "I will be a better man, a better husband, and a better laird for it."

She took his hand and looked him square in the eye. "But if yer father had not wrongly blamed ye, a wee bairn, for yer mother's death, then ye never would have met the blackguard, Brogan, in the first place."

"There is truth in yer words, but 'tis a truth my father would doubtless never hear. Where I am concerned, he is a hard man, hard and unforgiving."

He laid back down and opened his arms. She slid into his embrace, resting her cheek on his chest. "'Tis no wonder that I dreamt of her last night after these two days spent in quiet reflection."

She sat up a little, resting her chin in her hand. "Holy week is about forgiveness." A determined glint filled her eyes. "I love ye. Regardless of what yer past holds, ye're a good man." She smiled gently. "Ye can make a fresh start, Nathan. That is what Easter is all about, new beginnings."

He looked in her clear blue eyes, and in that moment, he believed the promise in her words. Pulling her close, he whispered. "With ye in my life, I feel like anything is possible."

Nathan closed his eyes and held his bride and prayed to find peace with the past. In his heart, he would always be of Clan Campbell. But he was also a Brodie now, and tomorrow he would celebrate Easter Sunday with his kin.

Nathan awoke the next morning with a new lightness in his heart as he gathered with his clan in the courtyard and sang hymns of praise. Then, he and Elora ushered the villagers into the chapel where Father Paul led them through a joyous Mass, filled with music. There was a liveliness in everyone's step. The spirit of celebration was infectious, and before too long, the real merrymaking began. The great hall was teeming with villagers as everyone gathered to prepare for the Easter feast.

As always, Elora ensured everything ran smoothly, but there was an ease in her manner that made Nathan's heart swell. Her quick laughter and bright eyes made it easy to forget the painful memories of the night before; that was, until Declan came charging into the great hall.

"Warriors, two dozen strong, ride this way!"

Elora's eyes flashed wide as she sought Nathan's gaze. "It must be Egan!"

"Nay," Declan said, crossing to their side. "They do not carry the colors of the Mackintosh," he said to Elora. Then he shifted his gaze to Nathan. "They wear the blue and green tartan of yer kin."

Nathan's nostrils flared. "Ye must be mistaken. How could they know I'm here?" Then his fists clenched. "Egan! He asked me from where I hailed. He must have alerted my father to my presence."

Elora's eyes flashed wide. "But why does he come?"

He shook his head. "I do not ken, but whatever his reason,

169

he does not come in peace." He turned to Declan. "Sound the alarm. See that every villager is within the castle grounds." Then, Nathan whirled around, heading toward the doors that led out to the courtyard.

"Where are ye going?" Elora called after him.

"I'm going to ride out to meet them."

She straightened her back and jutted out her chin. "I'm coming with ye."

He shook his head. "Nay, 'tis too dangerous."

She lifted her chin higher. "I wasn't asking yer permission."

He wanted to deny her, but he knew better than to demand her obedience. "All right. But ye must keep back and give me yer word that ye will turn back to the keep at the first sign of trouble."

She met his gaze and nodded. "Ye have my word."

As Nathan and Elora descended the castle steps to the courtyard, Caleb sat astride his mount. Beside him, two horses, saddled and ready, stomped at the ground.

Nathan's lips upturned slightly as he raised a brow at his friend. "Where do ye think ye're going?"

Caleb shrugged. "We're still partners, aren't we?"

Nathan smiled. "Aye, we are." Then he turned to Elora and lifted her onto Rosie. He looked her hard in the eye. "Remember yer promise."

"I will," she vowed, but then she cleared her throat and looked pointedly over his shoulder.

Nathan turned just as Declan and a band of warriors rode out of the stables. He threw his hands up. "I told ye already, Declan. I'm riding out to meet them alone."

Declan nodded. "Of course ye are, my laird, and we're going with ye."

Nathan locked eyes with the older man. Then his gaze shifted, taking in the Brodie warriors, Caleb, and his beautiful bride. Looking beyond them, he saw the villagers filling the courtyard, and in quick succession, they all dropped to one knee.

His chest tightened at the display of kinship. "Thank ye, my friends."

With a full heart, he mounted his horse and drew alongside Elora. "Together," he said.

She straightened in her saddle. "Together," she echoed. Then they nudged their horses forward and charged out the front gate. Racing through the empty village and fields, they crested the hill where they reined in their horses.

Declan drew his horse close to Nathan. "The rest of yer warriors are readying for battle, though I pray to God it does not come to that."

Nathan nodded grimly. Then he reached out and took Elora's hand. He met her clear blue gaze. Her eyes shone with strength. Taking a deep breath, he turned his gaze straight on. He had often wondered whether he would ever see Argyle Campbell again. And as the mighty din of horses thundering toward them reached his ears, he realized that he would soon be face to face with the very man who had banished him from his clan seven years ago.

Before too long, the Campbell warriors rode into view. He spied his father straightaway. A seasoned warrior, Argyle had thick black curls streaked with silver and broad shoulders.

"My father rides in lead," Nathan said out loud.

Nathan's gaze darted between the warriors flanking his father. To Argyle's right was his eldest brother, Matthew, whose black hair was pulled away from his face, revealing his thick sinewy neck and bare muscular shoulders, and to his father's left, was the middle brother, Peter, who was the tallest of them all and leanly built. Then, Nathan scanned the faces of the other warriors—he knew them all. Once upon a time, he had counted each one as his brother.

The Campbell warriors drew to a halt some feet away. Nathan locked eyes with his father's hard gaze. His heart raced as he released Elora's hand and took up his reins. For a moment, he felt uncertain, as if the child inside him and the man he was were at odds. But then he took a deep breath, narrowed his eyes on his father and nudged his horse forward, moving to the middle ground. He dismounted and withdrew his sword from the sheath strapped to his back and drove the tip of the blade into the ground. Then he stepped back and waited, his gaze never wavering from his father's silver eyes.

His weathered face impassive, the Campbell chieftain clicked his tongue and his horse stomped forward. Then he, too, dismounted. Nathan's nostrils flared as his father stepped toward him. Mirroring Nathan's movements, Argyle withdrew his own sword, but he let it fall to the ground as he charged at Nathan. Nathan tensed his stance, readying for his father's assault. Nearly upon him, his father raised both his arms. Then his silver eyes flooded with tears the instant before he pulled Nathan into a fierce embrace.

"My lad," his father rasped in his ear.

Bewildered, Nathan froze. He met Matthew's gaze over his father's shoulders, and his brother's silver eyes crinkled as a smile broke across his face.

In that moment, Nathan's heart swelled, and he wrapped his arms around his father and squeezed him with all his might. "Da," he blurted.

"My lad," Argyle exclaimed in a booming voice and lifted

Nathan's feet clear off the ground. "My lad!"

When Nathan's feet touched back down, his father gripped Nathan's shoulders. "We've looked everywhere for ye, my boy."

Nathan's mind raced. His heart pounded. "I...I don't understand."

A smile broke across Argyle's face and he stepped back. "Let me show ye something." Then he raised his hand. At his signal, Matthew and Peter nudged their horses, creating an opening so that Nathan could see the warriors on horseback behind them. And then, like drawing curtains to let in the light, the warriors diverged in opposite directions, making way for a cloaked rider with the hood pulled low over their eyes. Nathan stiffened as the rider reached up and slid their hood back, revealing the face of a striking woman with black curls and familiar blue eyes.

Nathan stumbled back with a gasp. Tears stung his eyes. He dropped to his knees and covered his face with his hands. "I must be dreaming." His voice broke.

Then, the sweetest sound he had ever heard reached his ears. "I am no dream, brother."

He dropped his hands away from his face. She stood in front of him. "Cait," he cried and leapt to his feet, sweeping her into his arms. "Ye're alive!" He spun her around and around. Her laughter rang out. Then he set her down and cupped her cheeks. "How can this be?"

Warmth flooded Cait's blue eyes. "I did not drown. I was washed ashore on the Isle of Arran and saved by a family of fishermen."

Nathan crushed her close again. "Praise be to all the angels." He drew away slightly and grazed the back of his fingers down her cheek. "Ye're a woman grown."

Cait nodded. "I am one and twenty, but I am still yer wee

lass," she smiled. "I always will be."

"My children," his father boomed, moving to stand beside them. His silver gaze locked with Nathan's. "I have regretted lashing out at ye long before we knew Cait was alive. There is so much I regret." His father's brows drew together. "But if ye can forgive me, I would like nothing more than to have all my children together again."

Nathan did not hesitate. He pulled his father close. "I love ye, Da." Then he drew away and seized Cait's hand. "There is someone I want ye to meet," he said as he led her to Elora's side.

Tears streaked his bride's cheeks. She slid to the ground, her blue eyes shining with joy.

Nathan turned to his sister. "Cait, meet my wife, Elora." His own voice broke as emotion surged up his throat. "Elora, meet my wee sister, back from the grave."

Fresh tears flooded Elora's gaze as she pulled Cait close. "Welcome, sister."

Nathan's breath hitched and he pulled them both into his arms. A moment later, his da came forward and wrapped his arms around them. Before too long, Matthew and Peter joined in, and then a cheer rose up among the surrounding warriors, both Brodie and Campbell.

"My laird," Declan called at length, drawing Nathan's gaze. "May I ride ahead and tell Murray and our warriors to stand down?"

"Aye," he answered. "And let Agnes know that we've more mouths to feed."

Everyone cheered again, and Elora cupped his cheek. Her gaze shone with love. "This will be an Easter feast the likes of which Castle Bròn has never seen!"

# Chapter Twenty One

Elora awoke to the feather soft caress of Nathan's lips making a trail of kisses down her throat to the hollow of her neck. "Good morrow," she rasped as she stretched her arms over her head. Blinking away the sleep from her eyes, she sought his gaze.

"Good morrow," he said, his voice husky. His hand curved over her bare breast. She closed her eyes and moaned softly as his thumb grazed her hard nipple.

"We mustn't," she said, gently pushing away his hand. "'Tis the morrow after Easter, and we have a castle filled with family—"

"And dozens of servants to see to their needs," he reminded her.

She gasped as his hand trailed over her hip. "They will be expecting us."

A seductive smile curved his lips. "We can be late." His fingers grazed her stomach, then parted her legs.

She gasped and threw her head back. "I'm never late."

"Never is a long time," he crooned and blew a stream of hot air against her inner thigh. She dug her fingers into his hair. Then his mouth found the heat of her, and all thoughts of duty fled her mind as his kiss made her body quiver and ache until

175

she cried out and shattered in his arms. Her chest heaving, he positioned himself between her thighs and entered her. She wrapped her legs around his waist and held on tight as he thrust deep inside her, again and again. Bound together by a love that would stand the test of time, they moved in passionate harmony until they both cried out, clinging to each other as waves of ecstasy rolled through them.

~ * ~

When, at last, they made their way down to the great hall, long after *Prime*, and took their rightful seats, Elora's cheeks burned as her kinfolk greeted them with knowing smiles.

"Good morrow, Daughter," Argyle said, as he stood and crossed to where she sat and pressed a fatherly kiss to her cheek. Then he placed his hand on Nathan's shoulders. "Good morrow, Son." Tears flooded the older man's gaze. "It does my heart good to say that."

Murray stood and cleared his throat. "I hate to be the bearer of ill tidings, but today is the morning after Easter."

Elora gave her steward a questioning look.

"The Lenten season is over," he said.

For a moment, she was puzzled, but then she drew a sharp breath and looked at Nathan. "Egan comes this day!"

"Ahh," Argyle chimed in. "Are ye speaking of Egan Mackintosh?"

She shifted her gaze to the senior Campbell. "The same."

The older man rubbed his chin. "I've been curious about Laird Mackintosh ever since we received his missive."

Elora turned to Nathan. "Ye were right. It was Egan who alerted yer father to yer whereabouts."

176

"What did his message contain?" Nathan asked, looking past her to meet his father's gaze.

"Some nonsense about ye claiming his rightful bride." Argyle lifted his shoulders. "I didn't pay much heed to the letter. As soon as I read that ye were at Castle Bròn, the rest was forgotten as I readied my men for our journey here."

"I'm confident there was little else of value in his message," Nathan said to his father before he turned to face Elora. He squeezed her hand reassuringly. "Do not fash yerself over his coming." He smiled at her. "Ye're my wife. Egan will just have to accept this."

Elora expelled the tension from her shoulders. Suddenly, she felt brighter. The weight of Egan's claim had been lifted from her shoulders. More than that, her people were safe, and the sovereignty of her clan was secured. She squared her shoulders and lifted her chin high. "Ye're right, Nathan." Then she turned back to her steward. "Let him come. He has no power here."

The morning meal commenced without further discussion of Egan. Elora watched as Tempest and Cait sat together, talking and laughing like old friends. She leaned close to Nathan. "Our sisters could be twins," she observed.

"Trust me. I've noticed," he said dryly before pressing a lingering kiss to her cheek.

Her gaze shifted back to the bustling hall. She waved to Allison as she waddled by. And then she smiled as she spotted Declan sitting with Hamish, playing a game of dice. Judging by the smile that stretched Hamish's creased face wide, the old man was winning. She continued to scan the happy faces when she suddenly realized that someone was missing.

She turned to Nathan. "Where is Caleb?"

"Alone, no doubt. He's been even more withdrawn lately."

177

Just as Elora was about to question Nathan further, the doors to the great hall swung open, and Caleb stormed into the room. His gaze locked with Nathan's. No words passed between the men who stood a room apart, but Nathan nodded at his friend before he leaned close to Elora and said, "Egan has arrived."

Caleb moved off to the side, and moments later Egan and half a dozen Mackintosh warriors thundered into the great hall. His head bent low, and his gaze fixed on Elora, Egan marched across the room.

"I'm here to witness yer nuptials," he sneered.

She fought to contain her triumphant smile. Slowly she stood, her composure intact. "Ye're late," she said simply.

With a snarl of rage, he shook his fist at her. "Ye have dishonored yer father's memory."

Tempest stood, her blue eyes flashing. "In life, my father dishonored every man, woman, and child in this room." Then she faltered and a smile curved her lips. "Well, all except for my brother-in-law's family. They had the great fortune of never knowing Cormag Brodie."

Nathan stood then. "In fact, I have to thank ye, Egan, for ye are the reason I have been reunited with my kin." Then he nodded at his brothers.

A thrill of victory shot up Elora's spine as she watched Nathan's older brothers, both imposing men, rise to their feet. Then they crossed to stand in between Egan and the high table. An instant later, Brodie and Campbell warriors alike stood and flanked Matthew and Peter.

"I also must thank ye," Tempest said as she, too, moved to stand alongside the men.

Elora tensed when her sister spoke up, but her worry eased when she observed Caleb drawing close until he stood just behind her.

"What have ye to thank me for?" Egan snarled at Tempest.

"For my new horse, of course," she answered sweetly, causing many of the villagers to chuckle.

Egan's face reddened as his gaze narrowed on Tempest. He started to walk toward her. "Clan Brodie has two ladies. Since yer sister has denied my rightful claim, 'tis only just that ye should take her place."

Tempest gasped, her eyes flashing wide.

"Ye go too far," Caleb snarled as he stepped in front of her, shielding her from Egan's sight. At the same time, the room erupted with protests in Tempest's defense.

"Egan Mackintosh," Elora said, her voice calling out above the sudden din of her angry kinfolk.

Egan whirled around and met her gaze, his face twisted in anger. "'Tis nothing more than my due," he shouted.

"Silence," she said, her voice booming. Her gaze bore into his. "Take yerself from Castle Bròn, and never return."

Egan opened his mouth to speak, but she thrust out her hand. "Ye have said yer piece. Unless ye wish to crawl out of here on yer belly like the snake ye are, then go before I allow my warriors to spill yer blood." Her eyes narrowed on him. "Make no mistake, Egan, every man in this room wants to be the one to send ye into the hereafter."

The sound of swords leaving their sheaths echoed through the great hall, as every Brodie and Campbell warrior readied themselves to carry out their lady's threat.

Nathan wrapped his arm around her shoulders. "Ye heard my wife. Be gone with ye!"

His face flushed, Egan bared his teeth and growled, but he turned on his heel. His men fell in line behind him as he marched from the great hall. When the door closed behind the enemy, the room erupted into cheers, but Elora could not celebrate. Her gaze was now fixed on Tempest's fearful face. She motioned for her sister, who hastened up the stairs to the high dais.

"Elora!" Tears of worry flooded Tempest's blue eyes.

"Nay, sweetling," Elora said, cupping her sister's cheek. "Ye needn't be afraid. He has no claim over ye. We are safe now, ye ken?"

Nodding bravely, Tempest threw her arms around her sister's neck. "Ye were amazing!"

"As were ye," Elora said, squeezing her sister tightly. Then she drew away. "Ye're a spirited lass and I love ye for it."

Cait rushed toward them, her black curls fanning out behind her. She pulled Tempest into a fierce hug. "Ye're so brave," Nathan's sister exclaimed.

Again, Elora marveled at how much they resembled each other.

"'Tis uncanny," Nathan said, appearing at her side. "They really could be twins." His gaze shifted to Elora. "But ye," he rasped, pulling her close. "Ye're one of a kind."

Her heart racing, she gazed lovingly into his silver eyes. "Ye're my kind of man." She wrapped her arms around his neck. "A renegade."

He laughed and pressed his forehead to hers. "Who would have known that an uptight noblewoman and a broken thief-taker could be so perfectly matched?" Then his face grew serious. "I was dead before ye, Elora," he whispered. "Ye've brought me back to life."

She wrapped her arms around his neck and brought her lips a breath from his. "Before ye, I never truly lived."

His lips claimed hers. He crushed her against his hard chest, and she gave herself over to the passion of his kiss as joy emanated from her unconstrained soul.

"I love ye," she said when their lips parted.

"And I love ye." Her heart quaked at the sight of his sensual sideways smile.

"Now, what are we to do?" Tempest asked, drawing Elora's gaze.

Elora smiled. "Now, we dance!"

Tempest and Cait clapped their hands with glee. The men gathered and moved the trestle tables aside. Then Clan Brodie and Clan Campbell came together and kicked up their heels in celebration of family, unity, and love everlasting.

Thank you for reading The Renegade! What's next?

Keep reading to find out!

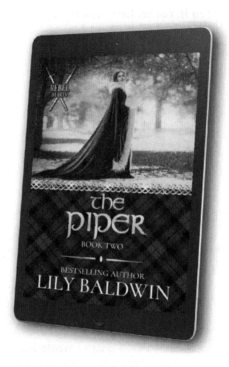

★★★★★ *"This story was wonderful. I truly enjoyed it right from the start."* ~ *Alison, Goodreads*

★★★★★ *"A...potent story that had me in tears...."* ~ *Eniko, Goodreads*

★★★★★ *"Amazing",* ~ *Emma, Goodreads*

★★★★★ *"A touching story, which will stay with me for a while."* ~ *NavyWavy 62, Bookbub*

**A laird whose sight has been stolen. A lady haunted by a tragic past. Together, can they escape the darkness?**

Hiding away in a castle tower overlooking snowswept moors, Lady Cait Campbell plays her pipe. Her music helps her deal with a past she can never forget and a world she now fears.

Gravely injured in battle, Laird Ewan MacLeod survives his wounds but loses his sight.  Believing himself incapable of protecting his people, he wishes to relinquish his chiefdom to his young brother who stubbornly refuses to accept the role, believing Ewan is still the rightful laird.

When their families come together to celebrate the Yuletide season, Ewan and Cait rekindle the friendship shared in their youth and the spark that has always existed between them ignites into a fiery attraction.

Still, love can only save them from their lonely fates if they both have the courage to face the challenges of the future, together.

*The Piper* is a Rebel Hearts novella.  Keep reading to enjoy a sample…

~ * ~

Lady Cait Campbell stood on a stool while Helen, her maid, knelt on the floor, pinning the hem of Cait's new tunic.

"This shade of plum is so becoming on ye, my lady," Helen said brightly as she paused to tuck a wayward lock of her own flaxen hair back into the knot piled on top of her head.

Cait felt her cheeks burn. "I'm certain 'tis not."

Helen cocked a brow at Cait. "One of these days, I'm going to pay ye a compliment, and ye're not going to protest or blush." Helen straightened her back and puffed out her chest. "Ye're going to stand proud and simply say, thank ye, Helen."

A pang of guilt struck Cait's heart. "I did not mean to appear ungrateful. I'm sorry. I—"

"Hush, pet," Helen crooned.  The stern set to her features softened as she stood, folding the Lady of Castle Shéan in her arms. "Ye didn't do anything wrong. I was just trying to encourage ye to…to…" The maid's words trailed off as she sighed. "I don't ken what I was trying to do." Helen lifted her shoulders. "All I ken is that I'm standing in the presence of the most beautiful, talented, and kindest lady in the Highlands, and no one would seek to contradict me on this point…except for ye." Helen's warm green eyes sought Cait's gaze.

Cait took a deep breath as she forced an impassive expression on her face all the while her stomach twisted, and fear made her chest ache. "I'm just…I'm nervous about…" She swallowed hard. "Yuletide is upon us…" Her knees felt like they were about to give out. "Please," she said, reaching for Helen's hand. "I must sit."

"My lady, ye're trembling!" Helen led Cait to a chair by the hearth. "Ye've gotten yerself in a right state, I can tell. And all my talk has not helped, I'd wager."

*Nothing helped. Everything hurt.*

Cait could hardly draw breath. "I…I just don't see why I need a new tunic."

Helen chuckled softly. "Bless ye, my lady. Is that all this is about? Yer father is a generous man as are yer brothers. They have no other lady to spoil but ye."

Cait held out the billowing sleeves of the costly Flemish wool she wore. "This is no simple garb. It might be something a bride would wear."

Helen sat down in the chair next to Cait and reached out, gently clasping her hands. "Look me in the eyes, my lady, and hear my words. They're not intending to marry ye off. Ye ken that yer family would never do that. They just want ye to have something especially lovely to wear for the upcoming festivities."

Cait's stomach dropped out. "I knew it." She clenched and unclenched her fists against the sensation that her fingers were going numb. "They want me to attend the feasts."

Helen's brows drew together. "Of course, they do, my lady. 'Tis Yule, after all."

Cait shot Helen a knowing look. "Do not pretend like ye don't know why I'm upset."

Helen shrugged with false casualness. "It won't be as bad as ye think."

Cait closed her eyes, trying to calm her racing heart. "Ye're probably right," she said weakly, although she knew Helen was mistaken.

A knock sounded at the door.

Cait stiffened.

Helen held out a soothing hand. "Ye're all right, my lady. Just breathe."

Incapable of breathing, Cait sat frozen while Helen crossed the room and opened the door. Her eldest brother entered the room.

Normally, when Matthew came to her chamber to visit with her, she was elated, but she knew this was not one of their usual visits.

Matthew's thick, curly black hair was pulled away from his handsome face, which shone with pride as he walked toward her. "Cait, ye're a vision!"

She managed to smile despite the knot of tears lodged in her throat, but judging by the way her brother's smile vanished, she knew she had failed to hide her trepidation.

"Kindly leave us, Helen," he said quietly to her maid.

Helen dipped in a quick curtsy, then hastened from the room; meanwhile, Matthew crossed to her side and claimed the chair next to hers. On another night, Cait would have giggled, watching her brother with his mighty shoulders, thick neck, and muscular thighs perch on the delicate high-backed chair near her hearth, but at that moment, she couldn't muster a spark of gaiety.

He leaned forward and covered her hands with his strong, calloused fingers. "Cait, have I ever put ye in harm's way?"

She met his silver gaze and shook her head.

"Laird Ewan MacLeod is a fine man, as is his mother and brother. Ye needn't fear them."

She shifted her gaze to the dancing flames, crackling in the hearth bed. "I do not fear them. I ken they mean me no harm. I just…I'm not comfortable meeting new people. And ye ken gatherings make me nervous—all those people, the din. Why can we just not celebrate as a family like we do every year?"

"Ewan is not a stranger to ye."

She raised a brow at her brother. "Matthew, I was eight when last he visited."

Matthew smiled, revealing the gap between his two front teeth. "Och, what a precocious lass ye were then, and how ye doted on Ewan. He was ten and five, and quick to laugh and make merry in those days." A distant look came into her brother's eyes as he chuckled softly. "I remember a Sabbath that was particularly stormy. Ye were frightened by the rumble of thunder. None of us could comfort ye but Ewan. He bundled ye up in his arms and rocked ye in a chair by the fire. He told ye stories, and ye sang together and laughed. Don't ye remember?"

Memories of a young man with golden hair and bright, cheerful eyes flashed in her mind. "I do," she said, lifting her shoulders. "But I am one and twenty now." She swallowed the knot of tears in her throat. "I'm not that precocious lass anymore."

Matthew looked her straight on. "Cait, ye can do this. I know ye can. Consider last spring when ye traveled with us all the way to Brodie territory and spent several days amidst a new clan."

"That was different," she said, crossing her arms over her chest. "I did that for Nathan so that our brother could see me in the flesh and know that I was alive after he believed me dead for so many years."

Matthew raked his hand through his hair. "I ken it was different."

"Nathan blamed himself for what happened to me," Cait added. "Father blamed him, too, at least in the beginning. 'Tis why I had to go—to help set things right between them. I would do anything for my family, even face my greatest fears." The mention of facing her fears made her heart beat faster. She could feel her panic grow, but she was careful not to show it.

Matthew sat back and expelled a slow breath. Cait could feel his mounting frustration. An instant later, he stood and took her hands and pulled her to her feet. "Look around ye, Cait." His voice held a note of urgency.

She did as he bade her. Her gaze settled on her four-poster bed with its blue quilt, dotted with white embroidered flowers. Then she scanned her walls, which were covered in tapestries made by her own hand. In that moment, a quiet delight entered her heart. The tapestries were vibrant with intricate patterns that told stories—some of which were true and heartbreaking, while others were forged within her own imagination and told of the woman she might have been if only she were stronger. Then her gaze settled on her bedside table where her pipe lay. It was her greatest treasure. When she played, her mind quieted, giving her soul reprieve from haunting memories that she otherwise couldn't escape.

"These walls are real," Matthew said, drawing her gaze as he placed his hand on the stones above the mantle. "Our keep is built on solid ground. Yer father is strong." He placed his hand on his heart. "As are yer brothers. We will never let harm befall ye again." He crossed to her side.

She swallowed hard. "I ken."

He knelt in front of her. "I ken ye know that. But knowing something and believing something are two different things. Ye must believe, Cait!"

She cast her gaze to the ground. "I know," she muttered. "I...I will try." The distant echo of screams came slowly to the fore of her mind, growing louder with every second, mocking her, proving to her that she would never forget. Tears stung her eyes.

"Look at me," Matthew beseeched her, his silver eyes pleading. "Seven years have passed since the ferry boat overturned and we thought we lost ye forever. But ye're safe now, Cait—safe and so dearly loved."

Despite how she tried to hold them back, her tears pushed past the confines of her lids. "I know."

Matthew pulled her close. "Believe, Cait," he whispered.

A hollow feeling settled in her chest. "I will try."

He pulled away slightly. A shadow crossed over his face. "Ewan is not the same man since he was wounded in battle. His family is worried, and so am I. I invited them to join us for Yule with the hope that coming together might lift his spirits. Ye know that we would never force ye, but please consider joining us at the high table when we welcome our guests." He pressed her hand to his heart. "For me, Cait."

She wanted to refuse him, to remain cloistered in her chamber where she could play her pipe and let the music wrap around her, blanketing her in beauty against the world she feared so much.

But the only thing greater than her fear was her love for her brothers.

"For ye, Matthew," she whispered.

A smile broke across his face as he scooped her into his muscular arms. "Thank ye, Cait!" He set her down quickly and cupped her cheeks. His eyes glinted with excitement. "Ye won't regret this. Ye'll see. This will be the most joyous Yuletide we've ever known."

Pasting a smile to her face, she gently pulled away from his touch. "I think I'll lie down for a while."

The exuberance in his posture and expression softened. A calm smile curved his lips. "I will leave ye then." He pressed a kiss to her cheek.

Her forced smile unwavering, she stood and watched his departure. When the door closed shut, she breathed out in a rush. Her heart pounded. Fear pulsed through her, inviting the sound of crashing waves, booming thunder, and endless screams to pummel her brain. Fighting the darkness that fought to consume her, she crossed to her bedside and picked up her pipe. Closing her eyes, she blew ribbons of melody that gently coiled around her, ethereal and as airy as a soft summer breeze. The beauty muffled the torment of her thoughts, until, at last, all she could hear was music.

The Piper is available in ebook and paperback.

Wishing you many blessings.

All my best,

Lily

Made in United States
Troutdale, OR
09/13/2023

12872986R10118